William Shakespeare's

The Taming of the Shrew
In Plain and Simple English

BookCaps Study Guides
www.bookcaps.com

Table of Contents

About This Series

The "Classic Retold" series started as a way of telling classics for the modern reader—being careful to preserve the themes and integrity of the original. Whether you want to understand Shakespeare a little more or are trying to get a better grasps of the Greek classics, there is a book waiting for you!

The series is expanding every month. Visit BookCaps.com to see all the books in the series, and while you are there join the Facebook page, so you are first to know when a new book comes out.

Characters

Persons in the Induction A LORD CHRISTOPHER SLY, a tinker HOSTESS PAGE PLAYERS

HUNTSMEN SERVANTS

BAPTISTA MINOLA, a rich man of Padua VINCENTIO, an old gentleman of Pisa LUCENTIO, son to

Vincentio; in love with Bianca PETRUCHIO, a gentleman of Verona; suitor to Katherina

Suitors to Bianca GREMIO HORTENSIO

Servants to Lucentio TRANIO BIONDELLO

Servants to Petruchio GRUMIO CURTIS

PEDANT, set up to personate Vincentio

Daughters to Baptista KATHERINA, the shrew BIANCA

WIDOW

Tailor, Haberdasher, and Servants attending on Baptista and Petruchio

SCENE: Sometimes in Padua, and sometimes in PETRUCHIO'S house in the country.

Play

Induction

Scene I
Before an alehouse on a heath

[Enter HOSTESS and SLY.]

SLY.
I'll pheeze you, in faith.

I'll hit you, I swear.

HOSTESS.
A pair of stocks, you rogue!

[A curse], you lowborn person!

SLY.
Y'are a baggage; the Slys are no rogues;
look in the chronicles: we came in with Richard
Conqueror. Therefore, paucas pallabris; let the
world slide. Sessa!

*You're very ignorant; the Slys are not lowborn;
look in the histories: we came [to England] with Richard
the Conqueror. Therefore, let the
world slide. Sessa!*

HOSTESS.
You will not pay for the glasses you have burst?

You will not pay for the glasses you have broken?

SLY.
No, not a denier. Go by, Saint Jeronimy,
go to thy cold bed and warm thee.

*No, not a penny. Go away, Saint Jeronimy,
go to your cold bed and get warm.*

HOSTESS.
I know my remedy;
I must go fetch the third-borough.

*I know what to do;
I must go fetch a policeman.*

[Exit.]

SLY.
Third, or fourth, or fifth borough, I'll answer
him by law. I'll not budge an inch, boy: let him
come, and kindly.

*No matter the policeman, I'll answer
him by law. I won't budge an inch, boy: let him
come, and gently.*

[Lies down on the ground, and falls asleep.]

[Horns winded. Enter a LORD from hunting, with Huntsmen and Servants.]

LORD.
Huntsman, I charge thee, tender well my
hounds;
Brach Merriman, the poor cur, is emboss'd,
And couple Clowder with the deep-mouth'd
brach.
Saw'st thou not, boy, how Silver made it good
At the hedge-corner, in the coldest fault?
I would not lose the dog for twenty pound.

*Huntsman, I command you, take good care of my
hunting-dogs;
Brach Merriman, the poor dog, is scratched,
And give Clowder something for his mouth.
Did you not see, boy, how Silver did well
At the corner of the hedge at the critical moment?
I would not lose that dog for twenty pounds.*

FIRST HUNTSMAN.
Why, Bellman is as good as he, my lord;
He cried upon it at the merest loss,
And twice to-day pick'd out the dullest scent;
Trust me, I take him for the better dog.

Why, Bellman is as good as he, my lord;
He howled at the slightest loss,
And twice today picked up the faintest scent;
Trust me, I consider him the better dog.

LORD.
Thou art a fool: if Echo were as fleet,
I would esteem him worth a dozen such.
But sup them well, and look unto them all;
To-morrow I intend to hunt again.

You are a fool: if Echo were as fast,
I would consider him worth a dozen such.
But feed them well, and look after them all;
To-morrow I intend to hunt again.

FIRST HUNTSMAN.
I will, my lord.

I will, my lord.

LORD.
[Sees Sly.]
What's here? One dead, or drunk?
See, doth he breathe?

What is this here? A man dead, or drunk?
See, does he breathe?

SECOND HUNTSMAN.
He breathes, my lord.
Were he not warm'd with ale,
This were a bed but cold to sleep so soundly.

If he were not warmed with alcohol,

This would be too cold a bed for him to sleep so
soundly.

LORD.
O monstrous beast! how like a swine he lies!
Grim death, how foul and loathsome is thine image!
Sirs, I will practise on this drunken man.
What think you, if he were convey'd to bed,
Wrapp'd in sweet clothes, rings put upon his fingers,

A most delicious banquet by his bed,
And brave attendants near him when he wakes,
Would not the beggar then forget himself?

Oh monstrous beast! He sleeps so much like a pig!
Grim death, how disgusting is your image!
Gentlemen, I will experiment on this drunken man.
What do you think, if he were taken to a bed,
Wrapped in the best of clothes, rings put on his
fingers,
And good servants near
him when he wakes,
Would the beggar not then forget who he was?

FIRST HUNTSMAN.
Believe me, lord, I think he cannot choose.

Believe me, lord, I think he cannot choose.

SECOND HUNTSMAN.
It would seem strange unto him when he wak'd.

It would seem strange to him when he woke.

LORD.
Even as a flattering dream or worthless fancy.
Then take him up, and manage well the jest.
Carry him gently to my fairest chamber,
And hang it round with all my wanton pictures;
Balm his foul head in warm distilled waters,
And burn sweet wood to make the lodging sweet.
Procure me music ready when he wakes,

Much like a dream or worthless fantasy.
Then take him up, and do a good job with the joke.
Carry him gently to my most beautiful room,
And decorate it with all my nudes;
Wash his disgusting head in warm, clean waters
And burn cedar to make the room smell good.
Get me music ready when he wakes,

To make a dulcet and a heavenly sound;
And if he chance to speak, be ready straight,

And with a low submissive reverence
Say 'What is it your honour will command?'
Let one attend him with a silver basin
Full of rose-water and bestrew'd with flowers;
Another bear the ewer, the third a diaper,
And say 'Will't please your lordship cool your hands?'

Some one be ready with a costly suit,
And ask him what apparel he will wear;
Another tell him of his hounds and horse,
And that his lady mourns at his disease.
Persuade him that he hath been lunatic;
And, when he says he is--say that he dreams,
This do, and do it kindly, gentle sirs;
It will be pastime passing excellent,
If it be husbanded with modesty.

FIRST HUNTSMAN.
My lord, I warrant you we will play our part,
As he shall think by our true diligence,
He is no less than what we say he is.

LORD.
Take him up gently, and to bed with him,
And each one to his office when he wakes.

[SLY is bourne out. A trumpet sounds.]

Sirrah, go see what trumpet 'tis that sounds:

[Exit SERVANT.]

Belike some noble gentleman that means,
Travelling some journey, to repose him here.

[Re-enter SERVANT.]

How now! who is it?

SERVANT.
An it please your honour, players
That offer service to your lordship.

LORD.
Bid them come near.

[Enter PLAYERS.]

To make a melodious and a heavenly sound;
And if he happens to speak, be ready straight away,
And with low, submissive respect
Ask, 'What is it your honor will command?'
Let one man serve him with a silver bowl
Full of rose-water and decorated with flowers;
Another carry the jug, the third a towel,
And ask, 'Will it please your lordship to cool your hands?'
Someone should be ready with expensive clothes,
And ask him what apparel he will wear;
Another tell him of his hounds and horse,
And that his wife is sad about his disease.
Persuade him that he has been a lunatic;
And, when he says he is--say that he dreams,
For he is nothing but a mighty lord.
It will be an excellent pastime,
If it is done carefully.

My lord, I promise you that we will play our part,
As he shall think by our true hard work,
That he is nothing other than what we say he says.

Pick him up gently, and take him to bed,
And each one do his job when he wakes.

[Sly is carried out. A trumpet blows.]

Sir, go see what trumpet it is that blows:

It is probably some noble gentleman that intends,
Traveling some journey, to rest here.

What's going on? Who is it?

If it pleases your honor, actors
That offer service to your lordship.

Tell them to come near.

Now, fellows, you are welcome.

PLAYERS.
We thank your honour.

LORD.
Do you intend to stay with me to-night?

PLAYER.
So please your lordship to accept our duty.

LORD.
With all my heart. This fellow I remember
Since once he play'd a farmer's eldest son;
'Twas where you woo'd the gentlewoman so well.
I have forgot your name; but, sure, that part
Was aptly fitted and naturally perform'd.

PLAYER.
I think 'twas Soto that your honour means.

LORD.
'Tis very true; thou didst it excellent.
Well, you are come to me in happy time,
The rather for I have some sport in hand
Wherein your cunning can assist me much.
There is a lord will hear you play to-night;
But I am doubtful of your modesties,
Lest, over-eying of his odd behaviour,--

For yet his honour never heard a play,--
You break into some merry passion
And so offend him; for I tell you, sirs,
If you should smile, he grows impatient.

PLAYER.
Fear not, my lord; we can contain ourselves,

Were he the veriest antick in the world.

LORD.
Go, sirrah, take them to the buttery,
And give them friendly welcome every one:
Let them want nothing that my house affords.

[Exit one with the PLAYERS.]

Sirrah, go you to Barthol'mew my page,
And see him dress'd in all suits like a lady;
That done, conduct him to the drunkard's chamber,

Now, fellows, you are welcome.

We thank your honour.

Do you intend to stay with me to-night?

If it pleases your lordship to welcome us.

With all my heart. This fellow I remember
Since he once played a farmer's eldest son;
It was where you wooed a noblewoman so well.
I have forgotten your name; but, surely, that part
Was suitably cast and naturally performed.

I think it was Soto that your honor means.

It is very true; you did an excellent job.
Well, you have come to me at a fortunate time,
For I would rather have some fun
Where your skills can help me a great deal.
There is a nobleman that will hear you act tonight;
But I am doubtful of your self-restraint,
In case, thinking excessively about his odd
behavior -
For his honor has never heard a play before -
That you start laughing
And in that way offend him; for I tell you, sirs,
If you smile, he will be irritated.

Don't worry, my lord; we can keep ourselves
contained,
Even if he were the funniest man in the world.

Go, sir, take them to the kitchen,
And give each of them a friendly welcome;
Let them lack nothing that my house can provide.

Sir, you should go to my page Bartholomew,
And dress him in lady's clothes;
That done, take him to the drunkard's room,

And call him 'madam,' do him obeisance.
Tell him from me--as he will win my love,--
He bear himself with honourable action,
Such as he hath observ'd in noble ladies
Unto their lords, by them accomplished;
Such duty to the drunkard let him do,
With soft low tongue and lowly courtesy,
And say 'What is't your honour will command,
Wherein your lady and your humble wife
May show her duty and make known her love?'
And then with kind embracements, tempting kisses,
And with declining head into his bosom,
Bid him shed tears, as being overjoy'd
To see her noble lord restor'd to health,
Who for this seven years hath esteemed him
No better than a poor and loathsome beggar.
And if the boy have not a woman's gift
To rain a shower of commanded tears,
An onion will do well for such a shift,
Which, in a napkin being close convey'd,
Shall in despite enforce a watery eye.
See this dispatch'd with all the haste thou canst;
Anon I'll give thee more instructions.

[Exit SERVANT.]

I know the boy will well usurp the grace,
Voice, gait, and action, of a gentlewoman;
I long to hear him call the drunkard husband;
And how my men will stay themselves from laughter

When they do homage to this simple peasant.
I'll in to counsel them; haply my presence

May well abate the over-merry spleen,
Which otherwise would grow into extremes.

[Exeunt.]

And call him 'madam,' treat him with respect.
Tell him from me – since this will gain my favor -
He carry himself with an honorable attitude,
Such has he has observed in noble ladies
Towards their husbands, by them accomplished;
Let him treat the drunkard in that way,
With soft, quiet words and humble courtesy,
And ask, 'What is it your honor will command,
So that your lady and your humble wife
May show her duty and prove her love?'
And then with kind hugs, tempting kisses,
And with a head resting on his chest,
Tell him to shed tears, as if overjoyed
To see her noble husband restored to health,
Who for these seven years has thought himself
No better than a poor and lowly beggar.
And if the boy does not have a woman's talent
To cry upon command,
An onion can help with that,
Which, hidden in a napkin,
Shall force the eyes to water anyway.
See this done with all the hurry you can;
And afterwards I'll give you more instructions.

I know the boy will do a good job faking the grace,
Voice, walk, and behavior, of a noblewoman;
I long to hear him call the drunkard 'husband';
And how my men will keep themselves from laughter
When they serve this simple peasant.
I'll be there to give them advice; hopefully my presence
May prevent an overly silly mood,
Which otherwise would become extreme.

Scene II
A bedchamber in the LORD'S house

[SLY is discovered in a rich nightgown, with ATTENDANTS: some with apparel, basin, ewer, and other appurtenances; and LORD, dressed like a servant.]

SLY.
For God's sake! a pot of small ale.

For God's sake! Give me some cheap beer.

FIRST SERVANT.
Will't please your lordship drink a cup of sack?

Will it please your lordship to drink a cup of fine wine?

SECOND SERVANT.
Will't please your honour taste of these conserves?

Will it please your honor to taste these preserves?

THIRD SERVANT.
What raiment will your honour wear to-day?

What clothes will your honor wear today?

SLY.
I am Christophero Sly; call not me honour nor lordship.
I ne'er drank sack in my life; and if you give me any
conserves, give me conserves of beef. Ne'er ask me
what raiment I'll wear, for I have no more doublets
than backs, no more stockings than legs, nor no more
shoes than feet: nay, sometime more feet than shoes,
or such shoes as my toes look through the over-leather.

*I am Christophero Sly; do not call me either
'honor' or 'lordship'. I never drank fine wine in
my life; and if you give me any preserves, give
me preserved beef. Never ask me what clothes I'll
wear, for I have no more doublets than I have
backs, no more stockings than I have legs, and
no more shoes than I have feet: actually,
sometimes I have more feet than I have shoes, or
the kind of shoes that my toes peek out from the
leather.*

LORD.
Heaven cease this idle humour in your honour!
O, that a mighty man of such descent,
Of such possessions, and so high esteem,
Should be infused with so foul a spirit!

*May Heaven stop this mood in your honor!
Oh, that a mighty man of such family,
So rich, and so well thought-of,
Should be filled with so terrible a spirit!*

SLY.
What! would you make me mad? Am not I Christopher
Sly, old Sly's son of Burton-heath; by birth a pedlar,
by education a card-maker, by transmutation a
bear-herd, and now by present profession a tinker?
Ask Marian Hacket, the fat ale-wife of Wincot, if she
know me not: if she say I am not fourteen pence on the
score for sheer ale, score me up for the lyingest knave
in Christendom. What! I am not bestraught. Here's--

*What! Would you make me appear insane? Am I
not Christopher sly, old Sly's son of Burton-heath;
by birth a peddler, by education a card-maker, by
fortune a bear-herder, and now by present
profession a mechanic? As Marian Hacket, the fat
lady barkeeper of Wincot, if she does no know me:
if she says I am not fourteen pence in debt for ale,
count me as the worst liar in all the Christian
lands. What! I am not in trouble. Here's –*

THIRD SERVANT.
O! this it is that makes your lady mourn.

Oh! This is what makes your wife sad.

SECOND SERVANT.
O! this is it that makes your servants droop.

Oh! This is what makes your servants depressed.

LORD.
Hence comes it that your kindred shuns your house,

As beaten hence by your strange lunacy.
O noble lord, bethink thee of thy birth,
Call home thy ancient thoughts from banishment,

And banish hence these abject lowly dreams.
Look how thy servants do attend on thee,
Each in his office ready at thy beck:
Wilt thou have music? Hark! Apollo plays,

It is because of this that your relatives avoid your house,
As driven away by your strange insanity.
Oh noble lord, think of your position,
Call home your former thoughts from where they have been sent away,
And send away there these pathetic lowly dreams.
Look how your servants serve you,
Each in his office ready at your beck and call:
Will you have music? Listen! [The Greek/Roman god of music] plays,

[Music]

And twenty caged nightingales do sing:
Or wilt thou sleep? We'll have thee to a couch
Softer and sweeter than the lustful bed
On purpose trimm'd up for Semiramis.
Say thou wilt walk: we will bestrew the ground:

Or wilt thou ride? Thy horses shall be trapp'd,
Their harness studded all with gold and pearl.
Dost thou love hawking? Thou hast hawks will soar

Above the morning lark: or wilt thou hunt?
Thy hounds shall make the welkin answer them
And fetch shall echoes from the hollow earth.

And twenty caged nightingales do sing:
Or will you sleep? We'll take you to a couch
Softer and sweeter than the luscious bed
Purposefully decked out for Semiramis.
Say you will walk: we will lay out a carpet on the ground.
Or will you ride? Your horses shall be decked out,
Their harnesses all studded with gold and pearls.
Do you love hunting with hawks? You have hawks that will soar
Higher than the morning lark: or will you hunt?
Your dogs shall make the sky answer them
And their howls shall echo from the hollow earth.

FIRST SERVANT.
Say thou wilt course; thy greyhounds are as swift
As breathed stags; ay, fleeter than the roe.

Say you will race; your greyhounds are as quick
As male deer; indeed, more nimble than female deer.

SECOND SERVANT.
Dost thou love pictures?
We will fetch thee straight
Adonis painted by a running brook,
And Cytherea all in sedges hid,
Which seem to move and wanton with her breath
Even as the waving sedges play with wind.

Do you love pictures?
We will fetch for you straightaway
Adonis painted by a running brook,
And Cytherea all hidden in the foliage,
Which seem to move and dance with her breath
The same way as the waving leaves play with wind.

LORD.
We'll show thee Io as she was a maid
And how she was beguiled and surpris'd,
As lively painted as the deed was done.

We'll show you Io as she was a young woman
And how she was tricked and surprised,
Painted like it is happening right in front of you.

THIRD SERVANT.
Or Daphne roaming through a thorny wood,
Scratching her legs, that one shall swear she bleeds

And at that sight shall sad Apollo weep,
So workmanly the blood and tears are drawn.

LORD.
Thou art a lord, and nothing but a lord:
Thou hast a lady far more beautiful
Than any woman in this waning age.

FIRST SERVANT.
And, till the tears that she hath shed for thee
Like envious floods o'er-run her lovely face,
She was the fairest creature in the world;
And yet she is inferior to none.

SLY.
Am I a lord? and have I such a lady?
Or do I dream? Or have I dream'd till now?
I do not sleep: I see, I hear, I speak;
I smell sweet savours, and I feel soft things:
Upon my life, I am a lord indeed;
And not a tinker, nor Christophero Sly.
Well, bring our lady hither to our sight;
And once again, a pot o' the smallest ale.

SECOND SERVANT.
Will't please your mightiness to wash your hands?

[Servants present a ewer, basin, and napkin.]

O, how we joy to see your wit restor'd!

O, that once more you knew but what you are!
These fifteen years you have been in a dream,
Or, when you wak'd, so wak'd as if you slept.

SLY.
These fifteen years! by my fay, a goodly nap.
But did I never speak of all that time?

FIRST SERVANT.
O! yes, my lord, but very idle words;
 For though you lay here in this goodly chamber,
Yet would you say ye were beaten out of door,
And rail upon the hostess of the house,
And say you would present her at the leet,
Because she brought stone jugs and no seal'd quarts.

Or Daphne roaming through a thorny wood,
Scratching her legs, that one shall swear she bleeds
And at that sight shall sad Apollo weep,
The blood and tears are drawn with such skill.

You are a lord, and nothing but a lord:
You are married to a lady for more beautiful
Than any other woman in these tough times.

And, until the tears she has shed for you
Like jealous floods overran her lovely face,
She was the most beautiful creature in the world;
And yet there are still none better than her.

Am I a lord? and have I such a lady?
Or am I dreaming? Or have I dreamed until now?
I do not sleep: I see, I hear, I speak;
I smell sweet scents, and I feel soft things:
Upon my life, I am a lord indeed;
And not a tinker, nor Christophero Sly.
Well, bring our lady here to see us;
And once again, a glass of the cheapest beer.

Will it please your mightiness to wash your hands?
[Servants present a jug, basin, and towel.]

Oh, how glad we are to see you come to your senses!
Oh, that you know once again who you are!
For the past fifteen years you have been dreaming,
Or, when you were awake, it was still as if you were sleeping.

For the past fifteen years! My, what a nap.
But did I never speak during all that time?

Oh yes, my lord, but very useless things;
For though you lay here in this good room,
Yet you would say you were chased outdoors,
And yell at the hostess of the house,
And say you would take her to court,
Because she did not bring the jugs you wanted.

Sometimes you would call out for Cicely Hacket.

SLY.
Ay, the woman's maid of the house.

THIRD SERVANT.
Why, sir, you know no house nor no such maid,

Nor no such men as you have reckon'd up,
As Stephen Sly, and old John Naps of Greece,
And Peter Turf, and Henry Pimpernell;
And twenty more such names and men as these,
Which never were, nor no man ever saw.

SLY.
Now, Lord be thanked for my good amends!

ALL.
Amen.

SLY.
I thank thee; thou shalt not lose by it.

[Enter the PAGE, as a lady, with ATTENDANTS.]

PAGE.
How fares my noble lord?

SLY.
Marry, I fare well; for here is cheer enough.

Where is my wife?

PAGE.
Here, noble lord: what is thy will with her?

SLY.
Are you my wife, and will not call me husband?
My men should call me lord: I am your goodman.

PAGE.
My husband and my lord, my lord and husband;
I am your wife in all obedience.

SLY.
I know it well. What must I call her?

LORD.
Madam.

Sometimes you would call out for Cicely Hacket.

Yes, the woman's maid of the house.

Why, sir, you have never known such a place or such a maid,
And no such men as you have imagined,
As Stephen Sly, and old John Naps of Greece,
And Peter Turf, and Henry Pimpernell;
And twenty more such names and men as these,
Which never existed, and no man ever saw.

Now, thank God for my recovery!

Amen.

I thank you; you will not lose by it.

How is my noble lord?

By Mary, I am doing well; for it is pleasant enough here.
Where is my wife?

Here, noble lord: what do you want with her?

Are you my wife, and will not call me husband?
My men should call me lord: I am your goodman.

My husband and my lord, my lord and husband;
I am your wife in all obedience.

I know it well. What must I call her?

Madam.

SLY.
Al'ce madam, or Joan madam?

Alice madam, or Joan madam?

LORD.
Madam, and nothing else; so lords call ladies.

Madam, and nothing else; that is what lords call ladies.

SLY.
Madam wife, they say that I have dream'd
And slept above some fifteen year or more.

Madam wife, they say that I have dreamed
And slept here some fifteen years or more.

PAGE.
Ay, and the time seems thirty unto me,

Being all this time abandon'd from your bed.

Yes, and that time has seemed like thirty years to me,
Having been all this time abandoned from your bed.

SLY.
'Tis much. Servants, leave me and her alone.
Madam, undress you, and come now to bed.

It it much. Servants, leave me and her alone.
Madam, get undressed, and come now to bed.

PAGE.
Thrice noble lord, let me entreat of you
To pardon me yet for a night or two;
Or, if not so, until the sun be set:
For your physicians have expressly charg'd,
In peril to incur your former malady,
That I should yet absent me from your bed:
I hope this reason stands for my excuse.

Three times noble lord, let me persuade you
To leave me alone for a night or two;
Or, if not, until the sun has set:
For your doctors have specifically commanded
To avoid risking you getting sick again,
That I should still stay away from your bed:
I hope this will be enough of an excuse.

SLY.
Ay, it stands so that I may hardly tarry so long;
but I would be loath to fall into my dreams again:
I will therefore tarry, in despite of the flesh and the
blood.

Yes, it is true that I can hardly wait so long;
but I would hate to start dreaming again:
I will therefore wait, despite my physical wants.

[Enter a SERVANT.]

SERVANT.
Your honour's players, hearing your amendment,
Are come to play a pleasant comedy;
For so your doctors hold it very meet,
Seeing too much sadness hath congeal'd your blood,

And melancholy is the nurse of frenzy:
Therefore they thought it good you hear a play,

And frame your mind to mirth and merriment,
Which bars a thousand harms and lengthens life.

Your honor's actors, hearing about your recovery,
Have come to play a pleasant comedy;
For your doctors consider it very suitable,
Seeing how too much sadness has chilled your blood,
And sadness leads to madness.
Therefore they thought it a good idea for you to see a play,
And put your mind into a cheerful mood,
Which prevents a thousand harms and lengthens life.

SLY.
Marry, I will; let them play it.

By Mary, I will;

Is not a commonty a Christmas gambold or a
tumbling-trick?

PAGE.
No, my good lord; it is more pleasing stuff.

SLY.
What! household stuff?

PAGE.
It is a kind of history.

SLY.
Well, we'll see't. Come, madam wife,
sit by my side and let the world slip:
we shall ne'er be younger.

[Flourish.]

*let them act it. Is 'commonty' a Christmas skit
or acrobatics?*

No, my good lord; it is more pleasing stuff.

What! household stuff?

It is a kind of history.

*Well, we'll see it. Come, madam wife,
sit by my side and let the world pass us by:
we shall never be younger.*

Act I

Scene I

Padua. A public place

[Enter LUCENTIO and TRANIO.]

LUCENTIO. Tranio, since for the great desire I had
To see fair Padua, nursery of arts,

I am arriv'd for fruitful Lombardy,
The pleasant garden of great Italy,
And by my father's love and leave am arm'd

With his good will and thy good company,
My trusty servant well approv'd in all,
Here let us breathe, and haply institute
A course of learning and ingenious studies.
Pisa, renowned for grave citizens,
Gave me my being and my father first,
A merchant of great traffic through the world,

Vincentio, come of the Bentivolii.
Vincentio's son, brought up in Florence,
It shall become to serve all hopes conceiv'd,
To deck his fortune with his virtuous deeds:
And therefore, Tranio, for the time I study,
Virtue and that part of philosophy
Will I apply that treats of happiness
By virtue specially to be achiev'd.
Tell me thy mind; for I have Pisa left
And am to Padua come as he that leaves

A shallow plash to plunge him in the deep,

And with satiety seeks to quench his thirst.

TRANIO.
Mi perdonato, gentle master mine;
I am in all affected as yourself;
Glad that you thus continue your resolve

To suck the sweets of sweet philosophy.
Only, good master, while we do admire
This virtue and this moral discipline,
Let's be no stoics nor no stocks, I pray;
Or so devote to Aristotle's checks
As Ovid be an outcast quite abjur'd.
Balk logic with acquaintance that you have,
And practise rhetoric in your common talk;

Tranio, because of the great desire I had
To see beautiful Padua, where the arts are
nurtured,
I have arrived for productive Lombardy,
The pleasant garden of great Italy,
And through my father's love and permission I am
supplied
With his goodwill and your good company,
My trusty servant with approval in all things,
Here let us breathe, and eventually establish
A course of learning and intelligent studies.
Pisa, well-known for wise citizens,
Was my birthplace,
A merchant of much buying and selling throughout
the world,
Vincentio, from the Betivoli family.
Vincentio's son, raised in Florence,
Shall be the one to bring all the hopes to reality,
To fill his life with his virtuous actions:
And therefore, Tranio, during the time I study,
Virtue and many forms of knowledge
I will go about in the kind of happiness
That you only get from being good.
Tell me what's on your mind; for I have left Pisa
And have come to Padua in the way of someone
who leaves
A shallow splash and then plunges into the deep
water,
And looks to satisfy his thirst.

Mi perdonato, my gentle master;
I am agreeing with you;
Glad that in this way you continue to be
determined
To fill yourself with the best of knowledge.
Only, my good master, while we are admiring
This virtue and this moral strength,
Let us please not be so serious and studious;
Or so devoted to dry information
That we completely abandon the arts.
Use logic that you know,
And practice rhetoric in your everyday talk;

Music and poesy use to quicken you;
The mathematics and the metaphysics,
Fall to them as you find your stomach serves you:
No profit grows where is no pleasure ta'en;
In brief, sir, study what you most affect.

LUCENTIO.
Gramercies, Tranio, well dost thou advise.
If, Biondello, thou wert come ashore,
We could at once put us in readiness,
And take a lodging fit to entertain
Such friends as time in Padua shall beget.

But stay awhile; what company is this?

TRANIO.
Master, some show to welcome us to town.

[Enter BAPTISTA, KATHERINA, BIANCA, GREMIO, and HORTENSIO. LUCENTIO and TRANIO stand aside.]

BAPTISTA.
Gentlemen, importune me no further,
For how I firmly am resolv'd you know;
That is, not to bestow my youngest daughter
Before I have a husband for the elder.
If either of you both love Katherina,
Because I know you well and love you well,
Leave shall you have to court her at your pleasure.

GREMIO.
To cart her rather: she's too rough for me.
There, there, Hortensio, will you any wife?

KATHERINA.
[To BAPTISTA]
I pray you, sir, is it your will
To make a stale of me amongst these mates?

HORTENSIO.
Mates, maid!
How mean you that? No mates for you,
Unless you were of gentler, milder mould.

KATHERINA.
I' faith, sir, you shall never need to fear;
I wis it is not halfway to her heart;
But if it were, doubt not her care should be

To comb your noddle with a three-legg'd stool,

Use music and poetry to make you lively;
The mathematics and the sciences,
Go to work on them as suits you best:
There is no profit where there is no pleasure;
To summarize, sir, study what suits you best.

Mercy, Tranio, you give very good advice.
If, Biondello, you were to come ashore,
We could at once be ready,
And rent a set of rooms fit to entertain
Such friends as we will make during our time in
Padua.
But just a moment; who are these people?

Master, some show to welcome us to town.

Gentlemen, do not plead with me any further,
For you know how firmly I have resolved;
To not let my youngest daughter marry
Before I have a husband for the elder.
If either of you both love Katherina,
Because I know you well and love you well,
You have permission to court her as you wish.

To cart her rather: she's too rough for me.
There, there, Hortensio, will you marry?

I'm asking you, sir, is it your intention
To make me a bargaining chip among these
mates?

Mates, young lady!
What do you mean by that? No mates
Unless you were a gentler, softer type.

In faith, sir, you shall never need to fear;
I know it is not halfway to her heart;
But if it were, have no doubt that her preference
would be
To comb your hair with a three-legged stool,

And paint your face, and use you like a fool.

HORTENSIO.
From all such devils, good Lord deliver us!

GREMIO.
And me, too, good Lord!

TRANIO.
Husht, master! Here's some good pastime toward:
That wench is stark mad or wonderful froward.

LUCENTIO.
But in the other's silence do I see
Maid's mild behaviour and sobriety.
Peace, Tranio!

TRANIO.
Well said, master; mum! and gaze your fill.

BAPTISTA.
Gentlemen, that I may soon make good
What I have said,--Bianca, get you in:
And let it not displease thee, good Bianca,
For I will love thee ne'er the less, my girl.

KATHERINA.
A pretty peat! it is best
Put finger in the eye, an she knew why.

BIANCA.
Sister, content you in my discontent.
Sir, to your pleasure humbly I subscribe:
My books and instruments shall be my company,
On them to look, and practise by myself.

LUCENTIO.
Hark, Tranio! thou mayst hear Minerva speak.

HORTENSIO.
Signior Baptista, will you be so strange?
Sorry am I that our good will effects Bianca's grief.

GREMIO.
Why will you mew her up, Signior Baptista,
for this fiend of hell,
And make her bear the penance of her tongue?

BAPTISTA.
Gentlemen, content ye; I am resolv'd.

And put makeup on your, and use you like a fool.

From all such devils, good Lord deliver us!

And me, too, good Lord!

Hush, master! Here's entertainment for us:
The rude woman is either insane or incredibly bold.

But in the other's silence I do see
A young woman's gentleness and calmness.
Quiet, Tranio!

Well said, master; be quiet, and feast your eyes.

Gentleman, so that I may soon make good
What I have said, - Bianca, get in:
And don't let it upset you, good Bianca,
For I will not love you any less, my girl.

A pretty speech! It would be better
To put a finger in the eye, and she would know why.

Sister, be content despite my lack of contentment.
Sir, I humbly obey your wishes:
My books and music will be my company,
To look upon them, and practice by myself.

Listen, Tranio! You may hear the chaste goddess of wisdom speak.

Sir Baptista, will you act so strangely?
I am sorry that our goodwill causes Bianca's grief.

Why will you hide her from men, Sir Baptista,
for the sake of this devil from hell,
And make her endure the punishment of her words?

Gentlemen, calm yourselves; my mind is made up.

Go in, Bianca.

[Exit BIANCA.]

And for I know she taketh most delight
In music, instruments, and poetry,
Schoolmasters will I keep within my house
Fit to instruct her youth. If you, Hortensio,
Or, Signior Gremio, you, know any such,
Prefer them hither; for to cunning men
I will be very kind, and liberal
To mine own children in good bringing up;
And so, farewell. Katherina, you may stay;
For I have more to commune with Bianca.

[Exit.]

KATHERINA.
Why, and I trust I may go too, may I not?

What! shall I be appointed hours, as though, belike,
I knew not what to take and what to leave? Ha!

[Exit.]

GREMIO.
You may go to the devil's dam: your gifts are so good
here's none will hold you. Their love is not so great,
Hortensio, but we may blow our nails together, and
fast it fairly out; our cake's dough on both sides.
Farewell: yet, for the love I bear my sweet Bianca,
if I can by any means light on a fit man to teach her
that wherein she delights, I will wish him to her father.

HORTENSIO.
So will I, Signior Gremio: but a word, I pray. Though
the nature of our quarrel yet never brooked parle,
know now, upon advice, it toucheth us both,--that we
may yet again have access to our fair mistress, and be
happy rivals in Bianca's love,--to labour and effect one
thing specially.

GREMIO.
What's that, I pray?

HORTENSIO.
Marry, sir, to get a husband for her sister.

GREMIO.
A husband! a devil.

Go in, Bianca.

And because I know she is most delighted
By music, instruments, and poetry,
I will keep good teachers inside my house
Suitable to instruct her youth. If you, Hortensio,
Or Sir Gremio, you, know any men like that,
Recommend them to me; for to talented men
I will be very kind, and generous
To my own children in good upbringing;
And so, farewell. Katherina, you may stay;
For I have more to discuss with Bianca.

Why, and I trust I am allowed to go too, may I
not?
What? Shall I be given hours, as though, perhaps,
I did not know what to take and what to leave?
Ha!

You may go to the devil's woman: your gifts are so
good that no one can hold you back. There love is
not so much, Hortensio, that we can't put our
differences aside. Farewell: yet, for the love I
have for my sweet Bianca, if I can in any way
come across a suitable man to teach her in the
things that she loves, I will recommend him to her
father.

So will I, Sir Gremio, but a word, please. Though
the type of quarrel we've had has never let us
negotiate before, know now, upon advice, that it
affects us both -- so that we may again have
access to our beautiful lady, and be happy rivals
in Bianca's love -- to work at and make happen
one thing especially.

What's that, I pray?

Indeed, sir, to get a husband for her sister.

A husband! a devil.

HORTENSIO.
I say, a husband.

GREMIO.
I say, a devil. Thinkest thou, Hortensio, though her father be very rich, any man is so very a fool to be married to hell?

HORTENSIO.
Tush, Gremio! Though it pass your patience and mine to endure her loud alarums, why, man, there be good fellows in the world, an a man could light on them, would take her with all faults, and money enough.

GREMIO.
I cannot tell; but I had as lief take her dowry with this condition: to be whipp'd at the high cross every morning.

HORTENSIO.
Faith, as you say, there's small choice in rotten apples. But, come; since this bar in law makes us friends, it shall be so far forth friendly maintained, till by helping Baptista's eldest daughter to a husband, we set his youngest free for a husband, and then have to't afresh. Sweet Bianca! Happy man be his dole! He that runs fastest gets the ring. How say you, Signior Gremio?

GREMIO.
I am agreed; and would I had given him the best horse in Padua to begin his wooing, that would thoroughly woo her, wed her, and bed her, and rid the house of her. Come on.

[Exeunt GREMIO and HORTENSIO.]

TRANIO.
I pray, sir, tell me, is it possible
That love should of a sudden take such hold?

LUCENTIO.
O Tranio! till I found it to be true,
I never thought it possible or likely;
But see, while idly I stood looking on,
I found the effect of love in idleness;
And now in plainness do confess to thee,
That art to me as secret and as dear
As Anna to the Queen of Carthage was,

I say, a husband.

I say, a devil. Do you think, Horensio, that even though her father is very rich, any man is so very a fool to be married to hell?

Pshaw, Gremio! Though it is beyond your patience and mine to endure her noisiness, why, man, there are enough good fellows in the world, and a man could come across them, who would take her with all her faults, and money enough.

I cannot tell; but I would be as likely to take her dowry with this condition: to be whipped at the city square every morning.

By my faith, as you say, there's very little choice in rotten apples. But, come; since this shared difficulty makes us friends, it shall remain friendly as long as it goes on, until by helping Baptista's eldest daughter to a husband, we set his youngest free for a husband, and then we can go back to our old rivalry. Sweet Bianca! It would be a happy man to get a reward like that! He that runs fastest wins the prize. What do you think of that, Sir Gremio?

I have agreed; and I would give him the best horse in Padua to begin his wooing, so that he would thoroughly woo and marry her, and rid the house of her. Come on.

*Please sir, tell me, is it possible
That love should take me so suddenly?*

*Oh Tranio! Until I discovered it to be true,
I never thought it possible or likely;
But see, while I stood idly looking on,
I found the beginning of love in idleness;
And now plainly confess to you,
Who is to me as precious and valuable
As Anna was to the Queen of Carthage,*

Tranio, I burn, I pine, I perish, Tranio,
If I achieve not this young modest girl.
Counsel me, Tranio, for I know thou canst:
Assist me, Tranio, for I know thou wilt.

TRANIO.
Master, it is no time to chide you now;
Affection is not rated from the heart:
If love have touch'd you, nought remains but so:

Redime te captum quam queas minimo.

LUCENTIO.
Gramercies, lad; go forward; this contents;

The rest will comfort, for thy counsel's sound.

TRANIO.
Master, you look'd so longly on the maid.

Perhaps you mark'd not what's the pith of all.

LUCENTIO.
O, yes, I saw sweet beauty in her face,
Such as the daughter of Agenor had,
That made great Jove to humble him to her hand,

When with his knees he kiss'd the Cretan strand.

TRANIO.
Saw you no more? mark'd you not how her sister

Began to scold and raise up such a storm
That mortal ears might hardly endure the din?

LUCENTIO.
Tranio, I saw her coral lips to move,
And with her breath she did perfume the air;
Sacred and sweet was all I saw in her.

TRANIO.
Nay, then, 'tis time to stir him from his trance.
I pray, awake, sir: if you love the maid,
Bend thoughts and wits to achieve her.
Thus it stands: Her elder sister is so curst and shrewd,

That till the father rid his hands of her,
Master, your love must live a maid at home;
And therefore has he closely mew'd her up,
Because she will not be annoy'd with suitors.

Tranio, I burn, I pine, I die, Tranio,
If I do not get this young, humble girl.
Give me advice, Tranio, for I know you can:
Help me, Tranio, for I know you will.

Master, it is no time to scold you now;
Affection is not judged by the heart:
If love has touched you, there is nothing else to do about it.

Redime te captum quam queas minimo.

Thank you, lad; go forward; this brings me contentment;
The rest will comfort, for your advice is solid.

Master, you looked so lengthily on the young woman.
Maybe you did not notice the drawback to it all.

Oh yes, I saw such sweet beauty in her face,
Like the daughter of Agenor had,
That made the great god Jove [Zeus] to humble himself to her hand,
When he kneeled upon the island of Crete.

Did you see no more? Did you not notice how her sister
Began to scold and cause such a commotion
That mortal ears could hardly endure the din?

Tranio, I saw her coral-colored lips move
And with her breath she perfumed the air;
Holiness and sweetness was all I saw in her.

No, then, it is time to wake him from his trance.
Please, wake up, sir: if you love the young lady,
Come up with some way to achieve her.
This is the situation: Her elder sister is so cursed and like a shrew,
That until his father gets rid of her,
Master, your love must live a virgin at home;
And therefore he has closely hidden her away,
Because she must not be annoyed with suitors.

LUCENTIO.
Ah, Tranio, what a cruel father's he!
But art thou not advis'd he took some care

To get her cunning schoolmasters to instruct her?

TRANIO.
Ay, marry, am I, sir, and now 'tis plotted.

LUCENTIO.
I have it, Tranio.

TRANIO.
Master, for my hand,
Both our inventions meet and jump in one.

LUCENTIO.
Tell me thine first.

TRANIO.
You will be schoolmaster,
And undertake the teaching of the maid:
That's your device.

LUCENTIO.
It is: may it be done?

TRANIO.
Not possible; for who shall bear your part
And be in Padua here Vincentio's son;
Keep house and ply his book, welcome his friends;
Visit his countrymen, and banquet them?

LUCENTIO.
Basta; content thee, for I have it full.
We have not yet been seen in any house,
Nor can we be distinguish'd by our faces
For man or master: then it follows thus:
Thou shalt be master, Tranio, in my stead,
Keep house and port and servants, as I should;
I will some other be; some Florentine,
Some Neapolitan, or meaner man of Pisa.
'Tis hatch'd, and shall be so: Tranio, at once
Uncase thee; take my colour'd hat and cloak.
When Biondello comes, he waits on thee;
But I will charm him first to keep his tongue.

[They exchange habits]

TRANIO.

Ah, Tranio, what a cruel father he is!
But did you not get something out of how he took
some care
To find her talented teachers to instruct her?

And, indeed, I am sir, and now it is planned.

I have it, Tranio.

Master, by my hand,
Both our imaginations meet and jump as one.

Tell me yours first.

You will be a teacher,
And go about the teaching of the young lady:
That's your plan.

It is: may it be done?

It is not possible; for who shall take your role
And be Vincentio's son here in Padua;
Take care of his affairs, welcome his friends;
Visit his relatives, and dine with them?

Enough; calm yourself, for I have the full plan.
We have not yet been seen in any house,
Nor is it obvious which of us is which
The servant and the master: so it follows this way:
You shall be master, Tranio, instead of me,
Keep house and harbor and servants, as I should;
I will be someone else; some man from Florence,
Some man from Naples, or a poorer man of Pisa.
It is planned, and it shall happen: Tranio, at once
Undress; take my colored hat and cloak.
When Biondello comes, he will serve you;
But I will trick him first to stay silent.

So had you need.
In brief, sir, sith it your pleasure is,
And I am tied to be obedient;
For so your father charg'd me at our parting,
'Be serviceable to my son,' quoth he,
Although I think 'twas in another sense:
I am content to be Lucentio,
Because so well I love Lucentio.

LUCENTIO.
Tranio, be so, because Lucentio loves;
And let me be a slave, to achieve that maid

Whose sudden sight hath thrall'd my wounded eye.

Here comes the rogue.

[Enter BIONDELLO.]

Sirrah, where have you been?

BIONDELLO.
Where have I been! Nay, how now! where are you?
Master, has my fellow Tranio stol'n your clothes?
Or you stol'n his? or both? Pray, what's the news?

LUCENTIO.
Sirrah, come hither: 'tis no time to jest,
And therefore frame your manners to the time.
Your fellow Tranio here, to save my life,
Puts my apparel and my count'nance on,
And I for my escape have put on his;
For in a quarrel since I came ashore
I kill'd a man, and fear I was descried.
Wait you on him, I charge you, as becomes,
While I make way from hence to save my life.
You understand me?

BIONDELLO.
I, sir! Ne'er a whit.

LUCENTIO.
And not a jot of Tranio in your mouth:
Tranio is changed to Lucentio.

BIONDELLO.
The better for him: would I were so too!

TRANIO.

As you had need.
Briefly sir, since it is your pleasure,
And I am commanded to be obedient;
For your father told be so at our separation,
'Be useful to my son,' he said,
Although I think it was in another sense:
I am content to be Lucentio,
Because I love Lucentio so well.

Tranio, do that, because Lucentio loves you too;
And let me be a servant, to achieve that young lady
Whose sudden sight has captured my wounded eye.
Here comes the rogue.

Where have you been, man?

Where have I been? What's going on? Master, has my fellow servant Tranio stolen your clothes? Or have you stolen his, or both? Please, what's the news?

Come here, man: this is no time to joke,
And therefore act appropriately for the situation.
Your fellow servant Tranio here, to save my life,
Puts on my clothes and expression,
And I have put on his in order to escape;
For in a quarrel since I came ashore
I killed a man, and I'm afraid I was recognized.
Serve him, I command you, as is correct,
While I run away from here to save my life.
You understand me?

I, sir! Not one bit.

And not one word of "Tranio" in your mouth:
Tranio has been changed to Lucentio.

The better for him: if only I were too!

So could I, faith, boy, to have the next wish after,

That Lucentio indeed had Baptista's youngest daughter.

But, sirrah, not for my sake but your master's, I advise

You use your manners discreetly in all kind of companies:
When I am alone, why, then I am Tranio;
But in all places else your master, Lucentio.

LUCENTIO.
Tranio, let's go. One thing more rests, that thyself execute, to make one among these wooers: if thou ask me why, sufficeth my reasons are both good and weighty.

[Exeunt.]

[The Presenters above speak.]

FIRST SERVANT.
My lord, you nod; you do not mind the play.

SLY.
Yes, by Saint Anne, I do. A good matter, surely: comes there any more of it?

PAGE.
My lord, 'tis but begun.

SLY.
'Tis a very excellent piece of work, madam lady: would 'twere done!

[They sit and mark.]

So could I, by my faith, boy, to have the next wish after,

That Lucentio indeed had Baptista's youngest daughter.

But, man, not for my sake but your master's, I advise

You use your manners discreetly when we have all kinds of company:
When I am alone, why, then I am Tranio;
But in all other places your master, Lucentio.

Tranio, let's go. There is one more thing for you to do yourself, to go among these wooers: if you ask me why, let it be enough for me to say I have good and strong reasons.

My lord, you are falling asleep; you are not paying attention to the play.

Yes, by Saint Anne, I am paying attention. A good story, surely: is there more to it?

My lord, it has only begun.

It is a very excellent piece of work, madam lady: if only it were finished!

[They sit and watch.]

Scene II

Padua. Before HORTENSIO'S house

[Enter PETRUCHIO and his man GRUMIO.]

PETRUCHIO.
Verona, for a while I take my leave,
To see my friends in Padua; but of all
My best beloved and approved friend,
Hortensio; and I trow this is his house.
Here, sirrah Grumio, knock, I say.

I leave Verona for a while,
To see my friends in Padua; but most of all
My best friend,
Hortensio; and I believe this is his house.
Here, Grumio, man, knock, I say.

GRUMIO.
Knock, sir! Whom should I knock?

Is there any man has rebused your worship?

Knock, sir! [He's misunderstood and thinks he's
supposed to hit someone.] Whom should I knock?
Is there any man who has [he means to say
'abused'] your worship?

PETRUCHIO.
Villain, I say, knock me here soundly.

Villain, I say, knock me here solidly.

GRUMIO.
Knock you here, sir! Why, sir, what am I, sir,
that I should knock you here, sir?

Knock you here, sir! Why, sir, what am I, sir,
that I should knock you here, sir?

PETRUCHIO.
Villain, I say, knock me at this gate;
And rap me well, or I'll knock your knave's pate.

Villain, I say, knock me at this gate;
And hit it well, or I'll hit you.

GRUMIO.
My master is grown quarrelsome.
I should knock you first,
And then I know after who comes by the worst.

My master is getting ready for a fight.
I should knock you first,
And then I know after who comes by the worst.

PETRUCHIO.
Will it not be?
Faith, sirrah, an you'll not knock, I'll ring it;
I'll try how you can sol, fa, and sing it.

Will it not be?
By my faith, man, if you won't knock, I'll ring it;
I'll try how you can sol, fa, and sing it.

[He wrings GRUMIO by the ears.]

GRUMIO.
Help, masters, help! my master is mad.

Help, someone, help! My master is insane.

PETRUCHIO.
Now, knock when I bid you, sirrah villain!

Now, knock when I tell you, villainous man!

[Enter HORTENSIO.]

HORTENSIO.
How now! what's the matter? My old friend Grumio!

and my good friend Petruchio!
How do you all at Verona?

What's going on? What's the matter? My old friend Grumio!
And my good friend Petruchio!
How do you all at Verona?

PETRUCHIO.
Signior Hortensio, come you to part the fray?
Con tutto il cuore ben trovato, may I say.

Sir Hortensio, have you come to stop the fight?
[Latin legal terms], may I say.

HORTENSIO.
Alla nostra casa ben venuto; molto honorato signor mio Petruchio.
Rise, Grumio, rise: we will compound this quarrel.

Alla nostra casa ben venuto; molto honorato signor mio Petruchio.
Stand, Grumio, stand: we will figure out this quarrel.

GRUMIO.
Nay, 'tis no matter, sir, what he 'leges in Latin. If this be not a lawful cause for me to leave his service, look you, sir, he bid me knock him and rap him soundly, sir: well, was it fit for a servant to use his master so; being, perhaps, for aught I see, two-and-thirty, a pip out?
Whom would to God I had well knock'd at first,
Then had not Grumio come by the worst.

No, it's nothing, sir, what he alleges in Latin. If this is not a lawful cause for me to leave his service, see, sir, he told me to knock him and rap him soundly, sir: well, was it appropriate for a servant to treat his master so; being, perhaps, for all I can see, thirty-two years older?
I wish to god I had hit him well at first,
Then Grumio would not have come by the worst.

PETRUCHIO.
A senseless villain!
Good Hortensio, I bade the rascal knock upon your gate,

And could not get him for my heart to do it.

A stupid villain!
Good Hortensio, I told the rascal to knock upon your gate,
And could not get him to do it no matter what.

GRUMIO.
Knock at the gate! O heavens!
Spake you not these words plain: 'Sirrah knock me here, rap me here, knock me well, and knock me soundly'?

And come you now with 'knocking at the gate'?

Knock at the gate! Oh heavens!
Did you not plainly say: 'Sirrah knock me here, rap me here, knock me well, and knock me soundly'?
And do you now come up with 'knocking at the gate'?

PETRUCHIO.
Sirrah, be gone, or talk not, I advise you.

Man, be gone, or be quiet, I advise you.

HORTENSIO.
Petruchio, patience; I am Grumio's pledge;
Why, this's a heavy chance 'twixt him and you,

Your ancient, trusty, pleasant servant Grumio.
And tell me now, sweet friend, what happy gale
Blows you to Padua here from old Verona?

Petruchio, patience; I will vouch for Grumio;
Why, this is just a misunderstanding between him and you,
Your elderly, trusty, pleasant servant Grumio.
And tell me now, sweet friend, what happy gale
Blows you to Padua here from old Verona?

PETRUCHIO.

Such wind as scatters young men through the world

To seek their fortunes farther than at home,
Where small experience grows.
But in a few, Signior Hortensio, thus it stands with me:
Antonio, my father, is deceas'd,
And I have thrust myself into this maze,
Haply to wive and thrive as best I may;
Crowns in my purse I have, and goods at home,
And so am come abroad to see the world.

HORTENSIO.
Petruchio, shall I then come roundly to thee
And wish thee to a shrewd ill-favour'd wife?

Thou'dst thank me but a little for my counsel;
 And yet I'll promise thee she shall be rich,
And very rich: but th'art too much my friend,
And I'll not wish thee to her.

PETRUCHIO.
Signior Hortensio, 'twixt such friends as we
Few words suffice; and therefore, if thou know

One rich enough to be Petruchio's wife,
As wealth is burden of my wooing dance,
Be she as foul as was Florentius' love,

As old as Sibyl, and as curst and shrewd
As Socrates' Xanthippe or a worse,
She moves me not, or not removes, at least,
Affection's edge in me, were she as rough

As are the swelling Adriatic seas:
I come to wive it wealthily in Padua;
If wealthily, then happily in Padua.

GRUMIO.
Nay, look you, sir, he tells you flatly what his mind is:
why, give him gold enough and marry him to a puppet
or an aglet-baby; or an old trot with ne'er a tooth in her
head, though she has as many diseases as two-and-fifty
horses: why, nothing comes amiss, so money comes
withal.

HORTENSIO.
Petruchio, since we are stepp'd thus far in,
I will continue that I broach'd in jest.
I can, Petruchio, help thee to a wife
With wealth enough, and young and beauteous;

Such wind as scatters young men through the world
To seek their fortunes farther than at home,
Where they can't get much experience.
But briefly, Sir Hortensio, this is my situation:
Antonio, my father, has died,
And I have brought myself to this city,
Possibly to get married and thrive as best I can;
I have money in my wallet, and goods at home,
And so have come abroad to see the world.

Petruchio, shall I then come around to you
And recommend to you a shrewish and unpleasant wife?
You would thank me very little for my advice;
And yet I'll promise you she shall be rich,
And very rich: but you are too good a friend,
And I won't introduce you to her.

Sir Hortensio, between such friends as we are
A few words are enough; and therefore, if you know
One rich enough to be Petruchio's wife,
As wealth is the point of my wooing dance,
Even if she was as disgusting as was Florentius' love,
As old as Sibyl, and as cursed and shrewish
As Socrates' wife Xanthippe or worse,
It does not affect me, at least
My ability to be affectionate, even if she was as rough
As the waves of the Adriatic are:
I come to marry wealthily in Padua;
If wealthily, then happily in Padua.

No, look, sir, he tells you flatly his opinion: why,
give him enough gold and marry him to a puppet;
or an old hag with no teeth, even if she has as
many diseases as fifty-two horses: why, nothing is
wrong with that, as long as money comes with it.

Petruchio, since we're on this subject,
I will explain that I was joking.
I can, Petruchio, help you get a wife
With enough wealth, and young and beautiful;

Brought up as best becomes a gentlewoman:
Her only fault,--and that is faults enough,--
Is, that she is intolerable curst
And shrewd and froward, so beyond all measure,
That, were my state far worser than it is,
I would not wed her for a mine of gold.

PETRUCHIO.
Hortensio, peace! thou know'st not gold's effect:
Tell me her father's name, and 'tis enough;
For I will board her, though she chide as loud

As thunder when the clouds in autumn crack.

HORTENSIO.
Her father is Baptista Minola,
An affable and courteous gentleman;

Her name is Katherina Minola,
Renown'd in Padua for her scolding tongue.

PETRUCHIO.
I know her father, though I know not her;
And he knew my deceased father well.
I will not sleep, Hortensio, till I see her;
And therefore let me be thus bold with you,
To give you over at this first encounter,
Unless you will accompany me thither.

GRUMIO.
I pray you, sir, let him go while the humour lasts.
O' my word, an she knew him as well as I do, she
would think scolding would do little good upon him.
She may perhaps call him half a score knaves or so;
why, that's nothing; and he begin once, he'll rail in his
rope-tricks. I'll tell you what, sir, an she stand him but
a little, he will throw a figure in her face, and so
disfigure her with it that she shall have no more eyes
to see withal than a cat. You know him not, sir.

HORTENSIO.
Tarry, Petruchio, I must go with thee,
For in Baptista's keep my treasure is:
He hath the jewel of my life in hold,
His youngest daughter, beautiful Bianca,
And her withholds from me and other more,
Suitors to her and rivals in my love;
Supposing it a thing impossible,
For those defects I have before rehears'd,
That ever Katherina will be woo'd:

Raised in the way a noblewoman should:
Her only fault,--and that is faults enough,--
Is that she is intolerably cursed
And shrewish and bold, so beyond all measure,
That, even if my situation was far worse than it is,
I would not marry her for an entire goldmine.

Horensio, enough! You do not know gold's effect:
Tell me her father's name, and it is enough;
For I will put up with her, even if she scolds as loud
As thunder when the clouds in autumn crack.

Her father is Baptista Minola,
A pleasant and polite nobleman;

Her name is Katherina Minola,
Well-known in Padua for her scolding tongue.

I know her father, though I do not know her;
And he knew my deceased father well.
I will not sleep, Hortensio, till I see her;
And thereroe let me be bold in this way with you,
To leave you behind for this first meeting,
Unless you will go with me there.

Please, sir, let him go while the mood lasts.
Upon my word, if she knew him as well as I do,
she would think scolding would do little good
when it came to him. She may perhaps call him a
dozen insults or so; why, that's nothing; and he'll
give as good as he gets. You don't know him, sir.

Wait, Petruchio, I must go with you,
For my treasure is in Baptista's castle:
He has the jewel of my life locked up,
His youngest daughter, beautiful Bianca,
And keeps her from me and others as well,
Suitors to her and rivals in my love;
Thinking it impossible,
For those flaws I mentioned earlier,
That Katherina will ever be wooed:

Therefore this order hath Baptista ta'en,
That none shall have access unto Bianca
Till Katherine the curst have got a husband.

GRUMIO.
Katherine the curst!
A title for a maid of all titles the worst.

HORTENSIO.
Now shall my friend Petruchio do me grace,
And offer me disguis'd in sober robes,
To old Baptista as a schoolmaster
Well seen in music, to instruct Bianca;
That so I may, by this device at least
Have leave and leisure to make love to her,
And unsuspected court her by herself.

GRUMIO.
Here's no knavery! See, to beguile the old folks,
how the young folks lay their heads together!

[Enter GREMIO, and LUCENTIO disguised, with books under his arm.]

Master, master, look about you: who goes there, ha?

HORTENSIO.
Peace, Grumio! 'tis the rival of my love.
Petruchio, stand by awhile.

GRUMIO.
A proper stripling, and an amorous!

GREMIO.
O! very well; I have perus'd the note.
Hark you, sir; I'll have them very fairly bound:
All books of love, see that at any hand,
And see you read no other lectures to her.
You understand me.
Over and beside Signior Baptista's liberality,
I'll mend it with a largess. Take your papers too,

And let me have them very well perfum'd;
For she is sweeter than perfume itself
To whom they go to.
What will you read to her?

LUCENTIO.
Whate'er I read to her, I'll plead for you,
As for my patron, stand you so assur'd,
As firmly as yourself were still in place;

	Therefore Baptista has decided,
	That none shall have access to Bianca
	Until Katherine the cursed as got a husband.
	Katherine the cursed!
	The worst possible title for a young woman.
	Now my friend Petruchio shall do me a favor,
	And present me disguised in formal robes,
	To old Baptista as a teacher
	Experienced in music, to instruct Bianca;
	That in this way I may, by this method at least
	Have permission and time to talk of love to her,
	And without being suspected court her by herself.
	Here's no trickery! See, to fool the old folks,
	how the young folks put their heads together!

Master, master, look around you: who goes there, huh?

Enough, Grumio! It is the rival of my love.
Petruchio, stand by awhile.

A proper young man, and one filled with romance!

Oh! Very well; I have read the note.
Listen, sir; I'll have them very beautifully bound:
All books of love, see that in any case,
And see you read no other lectures to her.
You understand me.
Beyond Signior Baptista's generosity,
I'll add to it with extra money. Take your papers too,
And let me have them very well perfumed;
For she is sweeter than perfume itself
The one they go to.

Whatever I read to her, I'll plead for you,
As for my employer, rest assured,
As firmly as you yourself were still in place;

Yea, and perhaps with more successful words
Than you, unless you were a scholar, sir.

GREMIO.
O! this learning, what a thing it is.

PETRUCHIO.
Peace, sirrah!

HORTENSIO.
Grumio, mum! God save you, Signior Gremio!

GREMIO.
And you are well met, Signior Hortensio.
Trow you whither I am going?
To Baptista Minola. I promis'd to enquire carefully

About a schoolmaster for the fair Bianca;
And by good fortune I have lighted well
On this young man; for learning and behaviour
Fit for her turn, well read in poetry
And other books, good ones, I warrant ye.

HORTENSIO.
'Tis well; and I have met a gentleman
Hath promis'd me to help me to another,
A fine musician to instruct our mistress:
So shall I no whit be behind in duty
To fair Bianca, so belov'd of me.

GREMIO.
Belov'd of me, and that my deeds shall prove.

GRUMIO.
[Aside.]
And that his bags shall prove.

HORTENSIO.
Gremio, 'tis now no time to vent our love:

Listen to me, and if you speak me fair,
I'll tell you news indifferent good for either.

Here is a gentleman whom by chance I met,
Upon agreement from us to his liking,
Will undertake to woo curst Katherine;
Yea, and to marry her, if her dowry please.

GREMIO.

Yes, and perhaps with more successful words
Than you, unless you were a scholar, sir.

O! this learning, what a thing it is.

Quiet, man!

Grumio, silence! God save you, Sir Gremio!

Good to see you, Sir Hortensio.
Can you guess where I am going?
To Baptista Minola. I promised to carefully ask around
About a good teacher for beautiful Bianca;
And by good fortune I have come across
This young man; for learning and behavior
Suitable for her, well-read in poetry,
And other books, good ones, I promise you.

It is good; and I have met a nobleman
Who has promised to help me to another,
A fine musician to instruct our lady:
So I shall in no way be behind in duty
To beautiful Bianca, I love so dearly.

That I love so dearly too, and that my actions shall prove.

And that his money shall prove.

Gremio, this is not a good time to discuss our love:
Listen to me, and if you are polite,
I'll tell you news that is impartially good for both of us.
Here is a gentleman whom I met by chance,
Upon an agreement between us that he likes,
Will go about wooing cursed Katherine;
Yes, and to marry her, if her dowry is pleasing.

So said, so done, is well. Hortensio,

have you told him all her faults?

PETRUCHIO.
I know she is an irksome brawling scold;
If that be all, masters, I hear no harm.

GREMIO.
No, say'st me so, friend? What countryman?

PETRUCHIO.
Born in Verona, old Antonio's son.
My father dead, my fortune lives for me;
And I do hope good days and long to see.

GREMIO.
O Sir, such a life, with such a wife, were strange!

But if you have a stomach, to't i' God's name;

You shall have me assisting you in all.
But will you woo this wild-cat?

PETRUCHIO.
Will I live?

GRUMIO.
Will he woo her? Ay, or I'll hang her.

PETRUCHIO.
Why came I hither but to that intent?
Think you a little din can daunt mine ears?
Have I not in my time heard lions roar?
Have I not heard the sea, puff'd up with winds,
Rage like an angry boar chafed with sweat?
Have I not heard great ordnance in the field,
And heaven's artillery thunder in the skies?
Have I not in a pitched battle heard
Loud 'larums, neighing steeds, and trumpets' clang?

And do you tell me of a woman's tongue,
That gives not half so great a blow to hear
As will a chestnut in a farmer's fire?
Tush, tush! fear boys with bugs.

GRUMIO.
[Aside]
For he fears none.

Said in that way, done in that way, is all good.
Hortensio,
have you told him all her faults?

I know she is an annoying brawling scold;
If that is all, gentleman, I see no harm in it.

No, you say, friend? Where are you from?

Born in Verona, old Antonio's son.
My father dead, my fortune lives for me;
And I do hope to live long and well.

Oh sir, such a life, with such a wife, would be strange!
But if you have the courage, go to it in God's name;
You shall have my assistance in everything.
But will you woo this wild-cat?

Will I live?

Will he woo her? Yes, or I'll hang her.

Why did I come here except with that intention?
Do you think a little din can daunt my ears?
Have I not in my time heard lions roar?
Have I not heard the sea, puffed up with winds,
Rage like an angry boar soaked with sweat?
Have I not heard explosions in the field,
And heaven's artillery thunder in the skies?
Have I not in a wild battle heard
Loud alarms, neighing horses, and the blast of trumpets?
And do you tell me of a woman's tongue,
That does not give half so big a noise
As will a roasting chestnut in a farmer's fire?
Pshaw! Boys frightened of bugs.

For he fears none.

GREMIO.
Hortensio, hark:
This gentleman is happily arriv'd,
My mind presumes, for his own good and ours.

HORTENSIO.
I promis'd we would be contributors,
And bear his charge of wooing, whatsoe'er.

GREMIO.
And so we will, provided that he win her.

GRUMIO.
I would I were as sure of a good dinner.

[Enter TRANIO, bravely apparelled;
and BIONDELLO.]

TRANIO.
Gentlemen, God save you! If I may be bold,
Tell me, I beseech you, which is the readiest way
To the house of Signior Baptista Minola?

BIONDELLO.
He that has the two fair daughters; is't he you mean?

TRANIO.
Even he, Biondello!

GREMIO.
Hark you, sir, you mean not her to--

TRANIO.
Perhaps him and her, sir; what have you to do?

PETRUCHIO.
Not her that chides, sir, at any hand, I pray.

TRANIO.
I love no chiders, sir. Biondello, let's away.

LUCENTIO.
[Aside]
Well begun, Tranio.

HORTENSIO.
Sir, a word ere you go.
Are you a suitor to the maid you talk of, yea or no?

TRANIO.

Hortensio, listen:
This gentleman is luckily arrived,
I believe, for his own good and ours.

I promised we would be sponsors,
And pay for his expenses, whatsoever.

And so we will, as long as he wins her.

I wish I were as certain of a good dinner.

[Enter TRANIO, well-dressed;
and BIONDELLO.]

Gentlemen, God save you! If I may be bold,
Tell me, I beg you, what is the quickest way
To the house of Sir Baptista Minola?

He that has the two beautiful daughters; is it he
you mean?

Yes him, Biondello!

Listen, sir, you don't mean to --

Perhaps him and her, sir; what are you going to
do about it?

Not the one that scolds, sir, in any case, please.

I have no fondness for scolders, sir. Biondello,
let's go.

Well begun, Tranio.

Sir, a word before you go.
Are you a suitor to the young lady you mention,
yes or no?

And if I be, sir, is it any offence?

GREMIO.
No; if without more words you will get you hence.

TRANIO.
Why, sir, I pray, are not the streets as free
For me as for you?

GREMIO.
But so is not she.

TRANIO.
For what reason, I beseech you?

GREMIO.
For this reason, if you'll know,
That she's the choice love of Signior Gremio.

HORTENSIO.
That she's the chosen of Signior Hortensio.

TRANIO.
Softly, my masters! If you be gentlemen,
Do me this right; hear me with patience.
Baptista is a noble gentleman,
To whom my father is not all unknown;
And were his daughter fairer than she is,

She may more suitors have, and me for one.
Fair Leda's daughter had a thousand wooers;

Then well one more may fair Bianca have;

And so she shall: Lucentio shall make one,
Though Paris came in hope to speed alone.

GREMIO.
What! this gentleman will out-talk us all.

LUCENTIO.
Sir, give him head; I know he'll prove a jade.

PETRUCHIO.
Hortensio, to what end are all these words?

HORTENSIO.
Sir, let me be so bold as ask you,
Did you yet ever see Baptista's daughter?

And if there is, sir, is there anything wrong with that?

No; if you will go away without saying any more.

*Why sir, I ask, are the streets not as free
For me as for you?*

But she is not as free.

For what reason, please tell me?

*For this reason, if you'll know,
That she's the chosen love of Sir Gremio*

That she's the chosen of Signior Hortensio.

*Softly, gentlemen! If you are nobles,
Treat me right this way; hear me with patience.
Baptista is a noble gentleman,
That knows my father;
And if her daughter were more beautiful than she is,
She may have many more suitors, and me for one.
Lovely Leda's daughter [Helen of Troy] had a thousand wooers;
So it's just as well that beautiful Bianca may have one more;
And so she shall: Lucentio shall become one,
Though Paris [Helen of Troy's lover] came hoping to be the only one.*

What! this gentleman will out-talk us all.

Sir, let him go ahead; I know he'll turn out to be a jade.

Hortensio, what is the point of all these words?

*Sir, let me be bold enough to ask you,
Have you ever seen Baptista's daughter?*

TRANIO.
No, sir, but hear I do that he hath two,
The one as famous for a scolding tongue
As is the other for beauteous modesty.

PETRUCHIO.
Sir, sir, the first's for me; let her go by.

GREMIO.
Yea, leave that labour to great Hercules,
And let it be more than Alcides' twelve.

PETRUCHIO.
Sir, understand you this of me, in sooth:
The youngest daughter, whom you hearken for,
Her father keeps from all access of suitors,
And will not promise her to any man
Until the elder sister first be wed;
The younger then is free, and not before.

TRANIO.
If it be so, sir, that you are the man
Must stead us all, and me amongst the rest;
And if you break the ice, and do this feat,
Achieve the elder, set the younger free
For our access, whose hap shall be to have her
Will not so graceless be to be ingrate.

HORTENSIO.
Sir, you say well, and well you do conceive;
And since you do profess to be a suitor,
You must, as we do, gratify this gentleman,
To whom we all rest generally beholding.

TRANIO.
Sir, I shall not be slack; in sign whereof,
Please ye we may contrive this afternoon,
And quaff carouses to our mistress' health;
And do as adversaries do in law,
Strive mightily, but eat and drink as friends.

GRUMIO, BIONDELLO.
O excellent motion! Fellows, let's be gone.

HORTENSIO.
The motion's good indeed, and be it so:--
Petruchio, I shall be your ben venuto.

[Exeunt.]

No, sir, but I hear that he has two,
And one is as famous for a scolding tongue
As the other is for beautiful humility.

Sir, sir, the first's for me; let her go by.

Yes, leave that task to great Hercules,
And let it be harder than the twelve Alcides gave
[Hercules].

Sir, understand this from me, in truth:
The youngest daughter, whom you desire,
Her father keeps away from all suitors,
And will not promise her to any man
Until the elder sister is first married;
The younger will then be free, and not before.

If it is true, sir, that you are the man
Who must help us all, and me among the rest;
And if you break the ice, and accomplish this task,
Achieve the elder, set the younger free
For our access, whose fate shall be to have her
Will not be so rude as to be ungrateful.

Sir, you speak well, and you think well too;
And since you announce yourself to be a suitor,
You must, as we do, gratify this gentleman,
To whom we are indebted.

Sir, I shall not be lacking; and to make a sign of it,
Please may we spend time together this afternoon,
And drink toasts to our ladies' health;
And act as rivals do in law,
Try hard against each other, but eat and drink as
friends.

Oh excellent idea! Fellows, let's go.

The idea is good indeed, and let it happen: --
Petruchio, I shall be your treat.

Act II

Scene I

Padua. A room in BAPTISTA'S house

[Enter KATHERINA and BIANCA.]

BIANCA.
Good sister, wrong me not, nor wrong yourself,

To make a bondmaid and a slave of me;
That I disdain; but for these other gawds,

Unbind my hands, I'll pull them off myself,
Yea, all my raiment, to my petticoat;
Or what you will command me will I do,
So well I know my duty to my elders.

Good sister, do not do me wrong, and do not wrong yourself either,
To make a servant girl and a slave of me;
That I disapprove of; but as for these other decorations,
Untie my hands; I'll pull them off myself,
Yes, all my clothes, down to my underwear;
Or I will do whatever you command me,
I know my duty to my elders that well.

KATHERINA.
Of all thy suitors here I charge thee tell
Whom thou lov'st best: see thou dissemble not.

Of all your suitors here, I order you to tell
Whom you love best: and don't lie to me.

BIANCA.
Believe me, sister, of all the men alive
I never yet beheld that special face
Which I could fancy more than any other.

Believe me, sister, of all the men alive
I have never yet seen that special face
Which I could desire more than any other.

KATHERINA.
Minion, thou liest. Is't not Hortensio?

Minion, you are lying. Is it not Hortensio?

BIANCA.
If you affect him, sister, here I swear I'll plead for you
myself but you shall have him.

If you are fond of him, sister, here I swear I'll
plead for you myself so you shall have him.

KATHERINA.
O! then, belike, you fancy riches more:
You will have Gremio to keep you fair.

Oh, then perhaps you desire riches more:
You will have Gremio to keep you beautiful.

BIANCA.
Is it for him you do envy me so?
Nay, then you jest; and now I well perceive
You have but jested with me all this while:
I prithee, sister Kate, untie my hands.

Is it because of him that you envy me so much?
No, that means you're joking; and now I can tell
You've only been joking with me all this time:
I beg you, sister Kate, untie my hands.

KATHERINA.
If that be jest, then an the rest was so.

If that is a joke, then the rest was too.

[Strikes her.]

[Hits her.]

[Enter BAPTISTA.]

BAPTISTA.
Why, how now, dame!
Whence grows this insolence? Bianca, stand aside.

Poor girl! she weeps. Go ply thy needle;
meddle not with her.
For shame, thou hilding of a devilish spirit,
Why dost thou wrong her that did ne'er wrong thee?
When did she cross thee with a bitter word?

Why, what's going on, woman?!
Where doest this rudeness come from? Bianca,
stand aside.
Poor girl! She cries. Go to your embroidery;
stop messing with her.
For shame, you offspring of an evil spirit,
Why do you wrong her that never did you wrong?
When did she ever insult or attack you?

KATHERINA.
Her silence flouts me, and I'll be reveng'd.

It is her silence that insults me, and I'll have my
revenge.

[Flies after BIANCA.]

[Chases after BIANCA.]

BAPTISTA.
What! in my sight? Bianca, get thee in.

What? Even when I'm watching! Bianca, go
inside.

[Exit BIANCA.]

KATHERINA.
What! will you not suffer me? Nay, now I see
She is your treasure, she must have a husband;
I must dance bare-foot on her wedding-day,
And, for your love to her, lead apes in hell.
Talk not to me: I will go sit and weep
Till I can find occasion of revenge.

What? Will you not endure me? No, now I see
She is your treasure, she must have a husband;
I must dance bare-foot on her wedding-day,
And, for your love of her, lead apes in hell.
Do not talk to me: I will go sit and cry
Until I can find a chance for revenge.

[Exit.]

BAPTISTA.
Was ever gentleman thus griev'd as I?
But who comes here?

Was a nobleman ever as troubled as I?
But who comes here?

[Enter GREMIO, with LUCENTIO in the habit of a
mean man; PETRUCHIO, with HORTENSIO as a
musician; and TRANIO, with BIONDELLO bearing
a lute and books.]

[Enter GREMIO, with LUCENTIO in the clothes
of a poor man; PETRUCHIO, with HORTENSIO
as a musician; and TRANIO, with BIONDELLO
carrying a lute and books.]

GREMIO.
Good morrow, neighbour Baptista.

Good day, neighbor Baptista.

BAPTISTA.
Good morrow, neighbour Gremio.
God save you, gentlemen!

Good day, neighbor Gremio.
God save you, gentlemen!

PETRUCHIO.

And you, good sir! Pray, have you not a daughter

Call'd Katherina, fair and virtuous?

BAPTISTA.
I have a daughter, sir, call'd Katherina.

GREMIO.
You are too blunt: go to it orderly.

PETRUCHIO.
You wrong me, Signior Gremio: give me leave.
I am a gentleman of Verona, sir,
That, hearing of her beauty and her wit,
Her affability and bashful modesty,
Her wondrous qualities and mild behaviour,
Am bold to show myself a forward guest
Within your house, to make mine eye the witness
Of that report which I so oft have heard.
And, for an entrance to my entertainment,
I do present you with a man of mine,

[Presenting HORTENSIO.]

Cunning in music and the mathematics,
To instruct her fully in those sciences,
Whereof I know she is not ignorant.
Accept of him, or else you do me wrong:
is name is Licio, born in Mantua.

BAPTISTA.
You're welcome, sir, and he for your good sake;
But for my daughter Katherine, this I know,

She is not for your turn, the more my grief.

PETRUCHIO.
I see you do not mean to part with her;
Or else you like not of my company.

BAPTISTA.
Mistake me not; I speak but as I find.

Whence are you, sir? What may I call your name?

PETRUCHIO.
Petruchio is my name, Antonio's son;
A man well known throughout all Italy.

BAPTISTA.

And you, good sir! Please tell me, don't you have a daughter
Called Katherina, beautiful and good?

I have a daughter, sir, call'd Katherina.

Your are too blunt: be more refined about it.

You wrong me, Sir Gremio: give me a chance.
I am a nobleman of Verona, sir,
That, hearing of her beauty and her intelligence,
Her pleasantness and humility,
Her wonderful qualities and quiet behavior,
Am bold enough to make myself a guest
Within your house, to make myself a witness
Of that report which I so often have heard.
And, in exchange for hosting me,
I now present you with one of my servants,

Clever in music and mathematics,
To instruct her fully in those fields,
Where I am aware she has some knowledge.
Accept him, or else you do me wrong:
His name is Licio, born in Mantua.

You're welcome, sir, and he is too for your sake;
Except when it comes to my daughter Katherine,
this I know,
She is not for you, I'm afraid.

I see you do not mean to separate from her;
Or else you do not like my company.

Do not misunderstand me; I only say what I
believe.
Where do you come from, sir? What is your name?

Petruchio is my name, Antonio's son;
A man well known throughout all Italy.

I know him well: you are welcome for his sake.

GREMIO.
Saving your tale, Petruchio, I pray,
Let us, that are poor petitioners, speak too.
Backare! you are marvellous forward.

PETRUCHIO.
O, pardon me, Signior Gremio; I would fain be doing.

GREMIO.
I doubt it not, sir; but you will curse your wooing.
Neighbour, this is a gift very grateful, I am sure of it.
To express the like kindness, myself, that have been
more kindly beholding to you than any, freely give
unto you this young scholar,
[Presenting LUCENTIO.]
that has been long studying at Rheims; as cunning in
Greek, Latin, and other languages, as the other in music
and mathematics. His name is Cambio; pray accept his
service.

BAPTISTA.
A thousand thanks, Signior Gremio; welcome,
good Cambio.-- [To TRANIO.]
But, gentle sir, methinks you walk like a stranger:
may I be so bold to know the cause of your coming?

TRANIO.
Pardon me, sir, the boldness is mine own,
That, being a stranger in this city here,
Do make myself a suitor to your daughter,
Unto Bianca, fair and virtuous.
Nor is your firm resolve unknown to me,
In the preferment of the eldest sister.
This liberty is all that I request,
That, upon knowledge of my parentage,
I may have welcome 'mongst the rest that woo,
And free access and favour as the rest:
And, toward the education of your daughters,
I here bestow a simple instrument,

And this small packet of Greek and Latin books:
If you accept them, then their worth is great.

BAPTISTA.
Lucentio is your name, of whence, I pray?

TRANIO.
Of Pisa, sir; son to Vincentio.

I know him well: you are welcome for his sake.

Save it, Petruchio, please,
Let us, that are poor beggars, speak too.
My goodness! You aren't very polite about it.

Oh, pardon me, Sir Gremio; I would rather be doing.

I do not doubt it, sir; but you will curse your wooing. Neighbor, this is a gift for which you will be very grateful, I am sure of it. To express similar kindness, myself, that have been kinder to you than any, I freely give to you this young scholar, [Presenting LUCENTIO.] that has studied at Rheims for a long time; he is as clever in Greek, Latin, and other languages, as the other is in music and mathematics. His name is Cambio; please accept his service.

A thousand thanks, Sir Gremio; welcome, g good Cambio. -- [To TRANIO.]
But, gentle sir, I think you walk like a stranger: may I ask why you have come here?

Pardon me sir, the boldness is my own,
That, being a stranger in this city here,
Do make myself a suitor to your daughter,
To Bianca, beautiful and virtuous.
And I am aware of your decision
In favor of the eldest sister.
This freedom is all that I request,
That, once you know of my family,
I may be welcome among the rest that woo,
And as much access and favor as the rest:
And, toward the education of your daughters,
I here give you the gift of a simple musical instrument,
And this small bag of Greek and Latin books:
If you accept them, then they have much worth.

Lucentio is your name, from where, may I ask?

Of Pisa, sir; son to Vincentio.

BAPTISTA.
A mighty man of Pisa: by report I know him well:
you are very welcome, sir.
[To HORTENSIO.]
Take you the lute,
[To LUCENTIO.]
and you the set of books;
You shall go see your pupils presently. Holla, within!

[Enter a SERVANT.]

Sirrah, lead these gentlemen
To my two daughters, and tell them both
These are their tutors: bid them use them well.

[Exit SERVANT, with HORTENSIO, LUCENTIO, and BIONDELLO.]

We will go walk a little in the orchard,
And then to dinner. You are passing welcome,
And so I pray you all to think yourselves.

PETRUCHIO.
Signior Baptista, my business asketh haste,
And every day I cannot come to woo.
You knew my father well, and in him me,
Left solely heir to all his lands and goods,
Which I have bettered rather than decreas'd:
Then tell me, if I get your daughter's love,
What dowry shall I have with her to wife?

BAPTISTA.
After my death, the one half of my lands,
And in possession twenty thousand crowns.

PETRUCHIO.
And, for that dowry, I'll assure her of
Her widowhood, be it that she survive me,
In all my lands and leases whatsoever.
Let specialities be therefore drawn between us,
That covenants may be kept on either hand.

BAPTISTA.
Ay, when the special thing is well obtain'd,
That is, her love; for that is all in all.

PETRUCHIO.
Why, that is nothing; for I tell you, father,
I am as peremptory as she proud-minded;
And where two raging fires meet together,
They do consume the thing that feeds their fury:

A mighty man of Pisa: I know him by reputation:
you are very welcome, sir.

You take the lute,

and you the set of books;
You shall go see your students in a moment. Hello,
you people inside!

My man, lead these noblemen
To my two daughters, and tell them both
These are their tutors: tell them to treat them well.

We will go walk a little in the orchard,
And then to dinner. You are most welcome,
And in that way I request all of you to consider
yourselves.

Sir Baptista, I have to hurry because of business,
And I cannot come to woo every day.
You knew my father well, and through him me,,
The only heir to all his lands and wealth,
Which I have made better rather than decreased:
Then tell me, if I get your daughter's love,
What dowry shall I have with her as my wife?

After my death, the one half of my lands,
And in possession twenty thousand crowns.

And, for that dowry, I'll promise her
As a widow, if she survives me,
In all my lands and property whatsoever.
Let a contract be therefore drawn up between us,
So that our agreements may be kept on both sides.

Yes, when the special thing is gotten,
That is, her love; for that is everything.

Why, that is nothing; for I tell you, father,
I am as strong-minded as she is haughty;
And where two raging fires meet together,
They eat up the thing that feeds their anger:

Though little fire grows great with little wind,
Yet extreme gusts will blow out fire and all;
So I to her, and so she yields to me;

For I am rough and woo not like a babe.

BAPTISTA.
Well mayst thou woo, and happy be thy speed!
But be thou arm'd for some unhappy words.

PETRUCHIO.
Ay, to the proof, as mountains are for winds,

That shake not though they blow perpetually.

[Re-enter HORTENSIO, with his head broke.]

BAPTISTA.
How now, my friend! Why dost thou look so pale?

HORTENSIO.
For fear, I promise you, if I look pale.

BAPTISTA.
What, will my daughter prove a good musician?

HORTENSIO.
I think she'll sooner prove a soldier:
Iron may hold with her, but never lutes.

BAPTISTA.
Why, then thou canst not break her to the lute?

HORTENSIO.
Why, no; for she hath broke the lute to me.
I did but tell her she mistook her frets,

And bow'd her hand to teach her fingering;
When, with a most impatient devilish spirit,
'Frets, call you these?' quoth she 'I'll fume with them';

And with that word she struck me on the head,
And through the instrument my pate made way;

And there I stood amazed for a while,
As on a pillory, looking through the lute;
While she did call me rascal fiddler,
And twangling Jack, with twenty such vile terms,

As she had studied to misuse me so.

Though a little fire grows larger with a little wind,
Yet extreme gusts will blow out fire and all;
I will be like that to her, and she will give in to me;
For I am rough and do not woo like a child.

May you woo well, and good luck!
But be prepared for some opposition.

Indeed, that will be the test, as mountains are for winds,
That do not shake even though they blow constantly.

[Re-enter HORTENSIO, with his head injured.]

What's going on, my friend? Why do you look so pale?

Because of fear, I promise you, if I look pale.

What, will my daughter turn out to be a good musician?

I think she'll sooner turn out to be a soldier:
Iron may survive her, but never lutes.

Why, then you cannot train her to the lute?

Why, no; for she has broken the lute on me.
I only told her she had made a mistake with her frets,
And bent her hand to teach her fingering;
When, with an extremely impatient, devilish spirit,
'Frets, you call these?' she asked, 'I'll fight with them';
And with those words she hit me on the head,
And my head went all the way through the instrument;
And I stood there amazed for a while,
As if in a set of stocks, looking through the lute;
While she called me a rascal fiddler,
And a twangling Jack, and twenty similar terrible insults,
As if she had studied to abuse me like that.

PETRUCHIO.
Now, by the world, it is a lusty wench!
I love her ten times more than e'er I did:
O! how I long to have some chat with her!

Now, by the world, that is a spirited girl!
I love her ten times more than I ever did:
Oh, how I long to talk with her!

BAPTISTA.
[To HORTENSIO.]
Well, go with me, and be not so discomfited;
Proceed in practice with my younger daughter;
She's apt to learn, and thankful for good turns.
Signior Petruchio, will you go with us,
Or shall I send my daughter Kate to you?

Well, go with me, and do not be so discouraged;
Go ahead and practice with my younger daughter;
She loves to learn, and is thankful for good turns.
Sir Petruchio, will you go with us,
Or shall I send my daughter Kate to you?

PETRUCHIO.
I pray you do. I will attend her here.

I request you do. I will meet her here.

[Exeunt BAPTISTA, GREMIO, TRANIO, and HORTENSIO.]

And woo her with some spirit when she comes.
Say that she rail; why, then I'll tell her plain
She sings as sweetly as a nightingale:
Say that she frown; I'll say she looks as clear
As morning roses newly wash'd with dew:
Say she be mute, and will not speak a word;
Then I'll commend her volubility,
And say she uttereth piercing eloquence:
If she do bid me pack, I'll give her thanks,
As though she bid me stay by her a week:
If she deny to wed, I'll crave the day
When I shall ask the banns, and when be married.

And woo her with some spirit when she comes.
Say that she yells; why, then I'll tell her plainly
She sings as sweetly as a nightingale:
Say that she frown; I'll say she looks as clear
As morning roses newly wash'd with dew:
Say she be mute, and will not speak a word;
Then I'll praise her clever talk,
And say she speaks piercing eloquence:
If she tells me to pack, I'll give her thanks,
As though she told me to stay with her a week:
If she refuses to marry, I'll ask the day
When I shall ask the priest, and when will we be
married.

But here she comes; and now, Petruchio, speak.

But here she comes; and now, Petruchio, speak.

[Enter KATHERINA.]

Good morrow, Kate; for that's your name, I hear.

Good morning, Kate; for that's your name, I hear.

KATHERINA.
Well have you heard, but something hard of hearing:
They call me Katherine that do talk of me.

You have heard well, but inaccurately,
Those that talk of me call me Katherine.

PETRUCHIO.
You lie, in faith, for you are call'd plain Kate,
And bonny Kate, and sometimes Kate the curst;
But, Kate, the prettiest Kate in Christendom,

Kate of Kate Hall, my super-dainty Kate,
For dainties are all cates: and therefore, Kate,
Take this of me, Kate of my consolation;
Hearing thy mildness prais'd in every town,

You lie, in faith, for you are called ordinary Kate,
And pretty Kate, and sometimes Kate the cursed;
But, Kate, the prettiest Kate in all the Christian
lands,
Kate of Kate Hall, my very dainty Kate,
For all Kates are dainties: and therefore, Kate,
Take this from me, Kate my comfort;
Hearing your gentleness praised in every town,

Thy virtues spoke of, and thy beauty sounded,
-- Yet not so deeply as to thee belongs,--

Myself am mov'd to woo thee for my wife.

KATHERINA.
Mov'd! in good time: let him that mov'd you hither

Remove you hence.
I knew you at the first,
You were a moveable.

PETRUCHIO.
Why, what's a moveable?

KATHERINA.
A joint-stool.

PETRUCHIO.
Thou hast hit it: come, sit on me.

KATHERINA.
Asses are made to bear, and so are you.

PETRUCHIO.
Women are made to bear, and so are you.

KATHERINA.
No such jade as bear you, if me you mean.

PETRUCHIO.
Alas! good Kate, I will not burden thee;
For, knowing thee to be but young and light,--

KATHERINA.
Too light for such a swain as you to catch;
And yet as heavy as my weight should be.

PETRUCHIO.
Should be! should buz!

KATHERINA.
Well ta'en, and like a buzzard.

PETRUCHIO.
O, slow-wing'd turtle! shall a buzzard take thee?

KATHERINA.
Ay, for a turtle, as he takes a buzzard.

Your virtues spoken of, and your beauty repeated,
-- Yet not so much as you actually turned out to have, --
I myself am moved to woo you for my wife.

Moved?! In good time: let him that moved you to here
Remove you from here.
I knew you from the first,
You were a moveable.

Why, what's a moveable?

A foot-stool.

You have hit on it: come, sit on me.

Asses are made to bear, and so are you.

Women are made to bear, and so are you.

No such fool as to bear you, if you mean me.

Too bad! Good Kate, I will not trouble you;
For, knowing you to be simply young and light, --

Too light for such a young man as you to catch;
And yet as heavy as my weight should be.

Should be?! Should buzz!

Well taken, and like a buzzard [vulture].

Oh, slowly moving turtle! Shall a buzzard take you?

Yes, for a turtle, as he takes a buzzard.

PETRUCHIO.
Come, come, you wasp; i' faith, you are too angry.

Come, come, you wasp; by my faith, you are too angry.

KATHERINA.
If I be waspish, best beware my sting.

If I am waspish, it would be best to watch out for my sting.

PETRUCHIO.
My remedy is, then, to pluck it out.

My cure for that, then, is to pull it out.

KATHERINA.
Ay, if the fool could find it where it lies.

Yes, if the fool could find it where it is.

PETRUCHIO.
Who knows not where a wasp does wear his sting?
In his tail.

Who does not know where a wasp has his sting? In his tail.

KATHERINA.
In his tongue.

In his tongue.

PETRUCHIO.
Whose tongue?

Whose tongue?

KATHERINA.
Yours, if you talk of tales; and so farewell.

Yours, if you talk of tales; and so farewell.

PETRUCHIO.
What! with my tongue in your tail? Nay, come again,
Good Kate; I am a gentleman.

What? With my tongue in your tail? No, try again, Good Kate; I am a gentleman.

KATHERINA.
That I'll try.

I'll test that.

[Striking him.]

PETRUCHIO.
I swear I'll cuff you if you strike again.

I swear I'll punch you if you hit again.

KATHERINA.
So may you lose your arms:
If you strike me, you are no gentleman;
And if no gentleman, why then no arms.

So you will lose your noble title: If you hit me, you are no gentleman; And if no gentleman, why then no coat of arms.

PETRUCHIO.
A herald, Kate? O! put me in thy books.

You are a herald, Kate? Oh! Put me in your books.

KATHERINA.
What is your crest? a coxcomb?

What is your family crest? A rooster's comb?

PETRUCHIO.
A combless cock, so Kate will be my hen.

A rooster with no comb, so Kate will be my hen.

KATHERINA.
No cock of mine; you crow too like a craven.

No rooster of mine; you crow too much like a coward.

PETRUCHIO.
Nay, come, Kate, come; you must not look so sour.

No, come on, Kate, come on; you must not look so sour.

KATHERINA.
It is my fashion when I see a crab.

It is my habit when I see a crab.

PETRUCHIO.
Why, here's no crab, and therefore look not sour.

Why, there is no crab here, and therefore do not look so sour.

KATHERINA.
There is, there is.

There is, there is.

PETRUCHIO.
Then show it me.

Then show it to me.

KATHERINA.
Had I a glass I would.

If I had a mirror I would.

PETRUCHIO.
What, you mean my face?

What, you mean my face?

KATHERINA.
Well aim'd of such a young one.

Well done for such a young one.

PETRUCHIO.
Now, by Saint George, I am too young for you.

Now, by Saint George, I am too young for you.

KATHERINA.
Yet you are wither'd.

Yet you are wrinkled.

PETRUCHIO.
'Tis with cares.

It's with worries.

KATHERINA.
I care not.

I don't care.

PETRUCHIO.
Nay, hear you, Kate: in sooth, you 'scape not so.

No, listen, Kate: in truth, you will not escape that way.

KATHERINA.
I chafe you, if I tarry; let me go.

I'll bother you, if I stay; let me go.

PETRUCHIO.
No, not a whit; I find you passing gentle.
'Twas told me you were rough, and coy, and sullen,
And now I find report a very liar;

No, not a bit; I find you very gentle.
I was told you were rough, and shy, and sullen,
And now I find reputation a liar;

For thou art pleasant, gamesome, passing courteous,
But slow in speech, yet sweet as spring-time flowers.
Thou canst not frown, thou canst not look askance,

Nor bite the lip, as angry wenches will,
Nor hast thou pleasure to be cross in talk;

But thou with mildness entertain'st thy wooers;
With gentle conference, soft and affable.
Why does the world report that Kate doth limp?
O sland'rous world! Kate like the hazel-twig
Is straight and slender, and as brown in hue
As hazel-nuts, and sweeter than the kernels.
O! let me see thee walk: thou dost not halt.

KATHERINA.
Go, fool, and whom thou keep'st command.

PETRUCHIO.
Did ever Dian so become a grove
As Kate this chamber with her princely gait?

O! be thou Dian, and let her be Kate,
And then let Kate be chaste, and Dian sportful!

KATHERINA.
Where did you study all this goodly speech?

PETRUCHIO.
It is extempore, from my mother-wit.

KATHERINA.
A witty mother! witless else her son.

PETRUCHIO.
Am I not wise?

KATHERINA.
Yes; keep you warm.

PETRUCHIO.
Marry, so I mean, sweet Katherine, in thy bed;

And therefore, setting all this chat aside,
Thus in plain terms: your father hath consented
That you shall be my wife your dowry 'greed on;
And will you, nill you, I will marry you.
Now, Kate, I am a husband for your turn;
For, by this light, whereby I see thy beauty,--

For you are pleasant, amiable, quite polite,
But quiet, yet sweet as the flowers of spring.
You cannot frown, you cannot look with disapproval,
Or bit your lip, as angry girls will,
And you do not take joy in being grumpy in conversation;
But with gentleness entertains your wooers;
With gentle conversation, soft and pleasant.
Why does the world report that Kate limps?
Oh slandering world! Kate is like the hazel-twig,
Straight and slender, and as brown in color
As hazelnuts, and sweeter than the kernels.
Oh, let me see you walk: you do not stagger.

Go away, fool, and whoever you command.

Did Diana [the Greek goddess] ever suit a grove
As much as Kate this room with her graceful walk?
Oh, you should be Diania, and let her be Kate,
And then let Kate be chaste, and Dian sportful!

Where did you study all these compliments?

It is spontaneous, from my mother-wit.

A witty mother! Her son is otherwise witless.

Am I not wise?

Yes; keep you warm.

Indeed, so I mean to, sweet Katherine, in your bed;
And therefore, enough with all this chatter,
Basically: your father has given permission
For you shall be my wife, your dowry agreed on;
And whether you like it or not, I will marry you.
Now, Kate, I am a husband for your type;
For, by this light, which allows me to see your beauty, --

Thy beauty that doth make me like thee well,--
Thou must be married to no man but me;
For I am he am born to tame you, Kate,
And bring you from a wild Kate to a Kate
Conformable as other household Kates.
Here comes your father. Never make denial;
I must and will have Katherine to my wife.

Your beauty that makes me like you a lot, --
You must be married to no man but me;
For I am the man born to tame you, Kate,
And bring you from a wild Kate to a Kate
As easy to deal with as other household Kates.
Here comes your father. Never say no;
I must and will have Katherine as my wife.

[Re-enter BAPTISTA, GREMIO, and TRANIO.]

BAPTISTA.
Now, Signior Petruchio,
how speed you with my daughter?

Now, Sir Petruchio,
how are you doing with my daughter?

PETRUCHIO.
How but well, sir? how but well?
It were impossible I should speed amiss.

How but well, sir? How but well?
It would be impossible for me to do poorly.

BAPTISTA.
Why, how now, daughter Katherine, in your dumps?

Why, what's going on, daughter Katherine, are
you down in the dumps?

KATHERINA.
Call you me daughter? Now I promise you
You have show'd a tender fatherly regard
To wish me wed to one half lunatic,
A mad-cap ruffian and a swearing Jack,
That thinks with oaths to face the matter out.

Do you call me your daughter? Now I promise you
You have showed a tender fatherly fondness
To wish me married to a half-crazy man,
A madcap troublemaker and a promising Jack,
That thinks to bluff his way through with oaths.

PETRUCHIO.
Father, 'tis thus: yourself and all the world
That talk'd of her have talk'd amiss of her:
If she be curst, it is for policy,
For she's not froward, but modest as the dove;
She is not hot, but temperate as the morn;
For patience she will prove a second Grissel,
And Roman Lucrece for her chastity;
And to conclude, we have 'greed so well together
That upon Sunday is the wedding-day.

Father, this is the situation: you and all the world
That have talked with her have been inaccurate:
If she is cursed, it is out of habit,
For she's pushy, but humble as a dove;
She is not hot, but as temperate as the morning;
She is as patient as Grissel,
And as chaste as the Roman Lucrece;
And to conclude, we have agreed so well together
That the wedding-day is on Sunday.

KATHERINA.
I'll see thee hang'd on Sunday first.

I would rather see you hanged on Sunday first.

GREMIO.
Hark, Petruchio; she says she'll see thee hang'd first.

Listen, Petruchio; she says she'd rather see you
hanged first.

TRANIO.
Is this your speeding? Nay, then good-night our part!

Is this how you're doing? No, then goodbye to our
part!

PETRUCHIO.
Be patient, gentlemen. I choose her for myself;

Be patient, gentlemen. I choose her for myself;

If she and I be pleas'd, what's that to you?
'Tis bargain'd 'twixt us twain, being alone,

That she shall still be curst in company.
I tell you, 'tis incredible to believe
How much she loves me: O! the kindest Kate
She hung about my neck, and kiss on kiss
She vied so fast, protesting oath on oath,
That in a twink she won me to her love.
O! you are novices: 'tis a world to see,

How tame, when men and women are alone,
A meacock wretch can make the curstest shrew.
Give me thy hand, Kate; I will unto Venice,
To buy apparel 'gainst the wedding-day.
Provide the feast, father, and bid the guests;
I will be sure my Katherine shall be fine.

BAPTISTA.
I know not what to say; but give me your hands.

God send you joy, Petruchio! 'Tis a match.

GREMIO, TRANIO.
Amen, say we; we will be witnesses.

PETRUCHIO.
Father, and wife, and gentlemen, adieu.
I will to Venice; Sunday comes apace;
We will have rings and things, and fine array;

And kiss me, Kate; we will be married o' Sunday.

[Exeunt PETRUCHIO and KATHERINA, severally.]

GREMIO.
Was ever match clapp'd up so suddenly?

BAPTISTA.
Faith, gentlemen, now I play a merchant's part,

And venture madly on a desperate mart.

TRANIO.
'Twas a commodity lay fretting by you;
'Twill bring you gain, or perish on the seas.

BAPTISTA.
The gain I seek is, quiet in the match.

If she and I are pleased, what's that to you?
It is still a bargain between the two of us, being alone,
That she shall still be rude in company.
I tell you, it is incredible to believe
How much she loves me: oh, the kindest Kate
She hung around my neck, and kiss upon kiss
She promised so fast, declaring oath on oath,
That in a blink she won me to her love.
Oh, you are inexperienced men: it is a world to see,
How tame, when men and women are alone,
A simple man can make the rudest woman.
Give me your hand, Kate; I will go to Venice,
To buy clothes for the wedding day.
Provide the feast, father, and invite the guests;
I will make sure my Katherine will be richly dressed.

I do not know what to say; but give me your hands.
God send you joy, Petruchio! It is a match.

Amen, we say; we will be witnesses.

Father, and wife, and gentlemen, see you soon.
I will go to Venice; Sunday comes soon;
We will have rings and things, and all sorts of riches;
And kiss me, Kate; we will be married on Sunday.

[Exit PETRUCHIO and KATHERINA, separately.]

Was a match ever slapped together so suddenly?

By faith, gentleman, I am acting like a merchant now,
And go out recklessly on a desperate bargain.

It was a commodity that was worrying you;
It will bring you rewards, or be lost on the seas.

The reward I hope for is quiet in the match.

GREMIO.
No doubt but he hath got a quiet catch.
But now, Baptista, to your younger daughter:
Now is the day we long have looked for;
I am your neighbour, and was suitor first.

TRANIO.
And I am one that love Bianca more
Than words can witness or your thoughts can guess.

GREMIO.
Youngling, thou canst not love so dear as I.

TRANIO.
Greybeard, thy love doth freeze.

GREMIO.
But thine doth fry.
Skipper, stand back; 'tis age that nourisheth.

TRANIO.
But youth in ladies' eyes that flourisheth.

BAPTISTA.
Content you, gentlemen; I'll compound this strife:
'Tis deeds must win the prize, and he of both

That can assure my daughter greatest dower
Shall have my Bianca's love.
Say, Signior Gremio, what can you assure her?

GREMIO.
First, as you know, my house within the city
Is richly furnished with plate and gold:
Basins and ewers to lave her dainty hands;
My hangings all of Tyrian tapestry;
In ivory coffers I have stuff'd my crowns;
In cypress chests my arras counterpoints,
Costly apparel, tents, and canopies,
Fine linen, Turkey cushions boss'd with pearl,

Valance of Venice gold in needle-work;
Pewter and brass, and all things that belong
To house or housekeeping: then, at my farm
I have a hundred milch-kine to the pail,
Six score fat oxen standing in my stalls,
And all things answerable to this portion.
Myself am struck in years, I must confess;
And if I die to-morrow this is hers,
If whilst I live she will be only mine.

No doubt but he has got a quiet catch.
But now, Baptista, to your younger daughter:
Now is the day we have waited for a long time;
I am your neighbor, and was a suitor first.

And I am the one that loves Bianca more
Than words can show or your thoughts can guess.

Youngling, you cannot love as preciously as I.

Graybeard, your love freezes.

But yours fries.
Kiddo, stand back; it is age that nourishes.

But youth in ladies' eyes that flourishes.

Be content, gentlemen; I'll add to this conflict:
It is actions that must win the prize, and he with both
That can assure my daughter a greater fortune
Shall have my Bianca's love.
Say, Signior Gremio, what can you assure her?

First, as you know, my house within the city
Is richly furnished with plate and gold:
Basins and sinks to wash her dainty hands;
My decorations are all of Tyrian tapestry;
I have stuffed my coins in ivory boxes;
My other goods in chests of cypress wood,
Expensive clothes, tents, and canopies,
Fine linen, Turkish cushions embossed with pearls,
Flag of Venice gold in needle-work;
Pewter and brass, and all things that belong
To house or housekeeping: then, at my farm
I have a hundred dairy cows being milked,
Twelve dozen fat oxen standing in my stables,
And all things answerable to this portion.
I myself am getting on in years, I must confess;
And if I die to-morrow this is hers,
If while I live she will be only mine.

TRANIO.
That 'only' came well in. Sir, list to me:
I am my father's heir and only son;
If I may have your daughter to my wife,
I'll leave her houses three or four as good
Within rich Pisa's walls as any one
Old Signior Gremio has in Padua;
Besides two thousand ducats by the year
Of fruitful land, all which shall be her jointure.
What, have I pinch'd you, Signior Gremio?

GREMIO.
Two thousand ducats by the year of land!
My land amounts not to so much in all:
That she shall have, besides an argosy
That now is lying in Marseilles' road.
What, have I chok'd you with an argosy?

TRANIO.
Gremio, 'tis known my father hath no less
Than three great argosies, besides two galliasses,

And twelve tight galleys; these I will assure her,
And twice as much, whate'er thou offer'st next.

GREMIO.
Nay, I have offer'd all; I have no more;
And she can have no more than all I have;
If you like me, she shall have me and mine.

TRANIO.
Why, then the maid is mine from all the world,
By your firm promise; Gremio is out-vied.

BAPTISTA.
I must confess your offer is the best;
And let your father make her the assurance,
She is your own; else, you must pardon me;
If you should die before him, where's her dower?

TRANIO.
That's but a cavil; he is old, I young.

GREMIO.
And may not young men die as well as old?

BAPTISTA.
Well, gentlemen, I am thus resolv'd.
On Sunday next, you know,
My daughter Katherine is to be married;

That 'only' is the point. Sir, listen to me:
I am my father's heir and only son;
If I may have your daughter to be my wife,
I'll leave her three or four houses as good
Within rich Pisa's walls as any one
Old Signior Gremio has in Padua;
Besides two thousand ducats by the year
Of good land, all which shall be her inheritance.
What, have I intimidated you, Sir Gremio?

Two thousand ducats by the year of land!
My land does not come to be worth that much;
That she shall have, besides a bunch of ships
That now is lying in Marseilles' road.
What, have I choked you with a bunch of ships?

Gremio, it is known that my father has no less
Than three huge groups of ships, besides more of
another kind of ship,
And twelve smaller boats; these I will promise her,
And twice as much, no matter what you offer next.

No, I have offered all; I have no more;
And she can have no more than all I have;
If you like me, she shall have me and mine.

Why, then the maid is mine from all the world,
By your solid promise; Gremio is outdone.

I must confess your offer is the best;
And let your father make her the assurance,
She is your own; else, you must pardon me;
If you end up dying before him, where is her
inheritance?

That's just nitpicking; he is old, I am young.

And may not young men die as well as old?

Well, gentleman, I have made my decision.
Next Sunday, you know,
My daughter Katherine is to be married;

Now, on the Sunday following, shall Bianca
Be bride to you, if you make this assurance;
If not, to Signior Gremio.
And so I take my leave, and thank you both.

GREMIO.
Adieu, good neighbour.

[Exit BAPTISTA.]

Now, I fear thee not:
Sirrah young gamester, your father were a fool
To give thee all, and in his waning age
Set foot under thy table. Tut! a toy!
An old Italian fox is not so kind, my boy.

[Exit.]

TRANIO.
A vengeance on your crafty wither'd hide!
Yet I have fac'd it with a card of ten.
'Tis in my head to do my master good:
I see no reason but suppos'd Lucentio

Must get a father, call'd 'suppos'd Vincentio';
And that's a wonder: fathers commonly
Do get their children; but in this case of wooing
A child shall get a sire, if I fail not of my cunning.

[Exit.]

Now, on the following Sunday, Bianca
Shall be your bride, if you make this promise;
If not, to Signior Gremio.
And so I take my leave, and thank you both.

Adieu, good neighbour.

Now, I am not afraid of you:
Young gambler, your father was a fool
To give you all, and in his declining years
Set food under your roof. Sheesh! A toy!
An old Italian fox is not so kind, my boy.

Revenge on your clever, wrinkled skin!
Yet I have bluffed you with a card of ten.
It is in my head to do my master good:
I see nothing for it but the man who's supposed to
be Lucentio
Must get a father, called 'supposed Vincentio';
And that's an amazing thing: fathers usually
Get their children; but in this case of wooing
A child shall get a father, if my cleverness does not
fail me.

Act III

Scene I

Padua. A room in BAPTISTA'S house

[Enter LUCENTIO, HORTENSIO, and BIANCA.]

LUCENTIO.
Fiddler, forbear; you grow too forward, sir.
Have you so soon forgot the entertainment
Her sister Katherine welcome'd you withal?

Fiddler, calm down; you are becoming rude, sir
Have you already forgotten the entertainment
Her sister Katherine welcomed you with earlier?

HORTENSIO.
But, wrangling pedant, this is
The patroness of heavenly harmony:

Then give me leave to have prerogative;
And when in music we have spent an hour,
Your lecture shall have leisure for as much.

But, arguing teacher, this is
The woman who appreciates and supports
heavenly harmony:
Then give me permission to go first;
And when we have spent an hour on music,
You will have time for a lecture that long.

LUCENTIO.
Preposterous ass, that never read so far
To know the cause why music was ordain'd!
Was it not to refresh the mind of man
After his studies or his usual pain?
Then give me leave to read philosophy,
And while I pause serve in your harmony.

Ridiculous fool, that never read far enough
To know why music was invented!
Was it not to refresh the human mind
After studies or usual work?
Then give me permission to read philosophy,
And when I take a break you can teach harmony.

HORTENSIO.
Sirrah, I will not bear these braves of thine.

Man, I will not endure these attempts of yours.

BIANCA.
Why, gentlemen, you do me double wrong,

Why, gentleman, you both wrong me,

To strive for that which resteth in my choice.
I am no breeching scholar in the schools,
I'll not be tied to hours nor 'pointed times,
But learn my lessons as I please myself.
And, to cut off all strife, here sit we down;
Take you your instrument, play you the whiles;
His lecture will be done ere you have tun'd.

To fight over what is actually up to me.
I am no young student in the schools,
I will not be tied to hours or appointed times,
But learn my lessons however it pleases me.
And, to stop this conflict, let us sit down here;
You take your instrument, play the scales;
His lecture will you be done before you have
tuned.

HORTENSIO.
You'll leave his lecture when I am in tune?

You'll leave his lecture when I am in tune?

[Retires.]

LUCENTIO.
That will be never: tune your instrument.

That will be never: tune your instrument.

BIANCA.
Where left we last?

Where did we stop before?

LUCENTIO.
Here, madam:--
Hic ibat Simois; hic est Sigeia tellus;
Hic steterat Priami regia celsa senis.

Here, madam:--
Hic ibat Simois; hic est Sigeia tellus;
Hic steterat Priami regia celsa senis.

BIANCA.
Construe them.

Explain them.

LUCENTIO.
'Hic ibat,' as I told you before, 'Simois,' I am Lucentio,
'hic est,' son unto Vincentio of Pisa, 'Sigeia tellus,'
disguised thus to get your love, 'Hic steterat,' and that
Lucentio that comes a-wooing, 'Priami,' is my man
Tranio, 'regia,' bearing my port, 'celsa senis,' that we
might beguile the old pantaloon.

'Hic ibat,' as I told you before, 'Simois,' I am
Lucentio, 'hic est,' the son of Vincentio of Pisa,
'Sigeia tellis,' disguised this way to get your love,
'Hic steterat,' and that Lucentio that is wooing,
'Priami,' is my servant Tranio, 'regia,' wearing my
clothes, 'celsa senis,' so that we may trick the old
father of yours.

HORTENSIO.
[Returning.] Madam, my instrument's in tune.

[Returning.] Madam, my instrument's in tune.

BIANCA.
Let's hear.--

Let's hear.--

[HORTENSIO plays.]

O fie! the treble jars.

Oh dear! The treble sounds awful.

LUCENTIO.
Spit in the hole, man, and tune again.

Spit in the hole, man, and tune again.

BIANCA.
Now let me see if I can construe it: 'Hic ibat Simois,'
I know you not; 'hic est Sigeia tellus,' I trust you not;
'Hic steterat Priami,' take heed he hear us not; 'regia,'
presume not; 'celsa senis,' despair not.

Now let me see if I can explain it: 'Hic ibat
Simois,' I do not know you; 'hic est Sigeia tullus,'
I do not trust you; 'Hic steterate Priami,' make
sure he does not hear us; 'regia' don't make false
assumptions; 'celsa senis,' but do not despair.

HORTENSIO.
Madam, 'tis now in tune.

Madam, it is now in tune.

LUCENTIO.
All but the base.

All but the base.

HORTENSIO.
The base is right; 'tis the base knave that jars. How
fiery and forward our pedant is!
[Aside]
Now, for my life, the knave doth court my love:
Pedascule, I'll watch you better yet.

The base is fine; it is the base troublemaker that
upsets things. How fiery and bold our teacher is!
[Aside]
Now, for my life, the troublemaker is courting my
love: little teacher, I'll watch you better yet.

BIANCA.
In time I may believe, yet I mistrust.

Eventually I may believe, yet I distrust.

LUCENTIO.
Mistrust it not; for sure, A Eacides Was Ajax,
call'd so from his grandfather.

Do not distrust it; for it is as true as Eacides was Ajax, named after his grandfather.

BIANCA.
I must believe my Master; else,

I must believe my Master; otherwise,

I promise you, I should be arguing still upon that doubt;

I promise you, I would still be arguing on that point;

But let it rest. Now, Licio, to you.
Good master, take it not unkindly, pray,
That I have been thus pleasant with you both.

But let it rest. Now, Licio, to you.
Good teacher, please do not be troubled
That I have acted pleasantly with you both.

HORTENSIO.
[To LUCENTIO]
You may go walk and give me leave awhile;
My lessons make no music in three parts.

You may go walk and leave me alone for a while;
My lessons make no music in three parts.

LUCENTIO.
Are you so formal, sir?
[Aside]
Well, I must wait,
And watch withal; for, but I be deceiv'd,
Our fine musician groweth amorous.

Are you so formal, sir?

Well, I must wait,
And watch all the while; for, unless I am mistaken,
Our fine musician is becoming romantic.

HORTENSIO.
Madam, before you touch the instrument,
To learn the order of my fingering,
I must begin with rudiments of art;
To teach you gamut in a briefer sort,
More pleasant, pithy, and effectual,
Than hath been taught by any of my trade:

And there it is in writing, fairly drawn.

Madam, before you touch the instrument,
To learn the way I teach fingering,
I must begin with the basics of art;
To teach you the basics in a briefer way,
More pleasant, short, and effective,
Than it has been taught by any other music teacher:
And there it is in writing, fairly drawn.

BIANCA.
Why, I am past my gamut long ago.

Why, I learned the basics long ago.

HORTENSIO.
Yet read the gamut of Hortensio.

Yet read the gamut of Hortensio.

BIANCA.
'Gamut' I am, the ground of all accord, 'A re,' to plead
Hortensio's passion; 'B mi,' Bianca, take him for thy
lord, 'C fa ut,' that loves with all affection:
'D sol re,' one clef, two notes have I 'E la mi,'
show pity or I die.

'Gamut' I am, the foundation of all harmony,
'A re,' to beg for Hortensio's love; 'B mi,' Bianca,
marry him, 'C fa ut,' that loves with all affection:
'D sol re,' one clef, two notes I have 'E la me,'
show pity or I will die.

Call you this gamut? Tut, I like it not:
Old fashions please me best; I am not so nice,
To change true rules for odd inventions.

[Enter a SERVANT.]

SERVANT.
Mistress, your father prays you leave your books,

And help to dress your sister's chamber up:
You know to-morrow is the wedding-day.

BIANCA.
Farewell, sweet masters, both: I must be gone.

[Exeunt BIANCA and SERVANT.]

LUCENTIO.
Faith, mistress, then I have no cause to stay.

[Exit.]

HORTENSIO.
But I have cause to pry into this pedant:
Methinks he looks as though he were in love.
Yet if thy thoughts, Bianca, be so humble
To cast thy wand'ring eyes on every stale,
Seize thee that list: if once I find thee ranging,
Hortensio will be quit with thee by changing.

[Exit.]

You call this basic? Hm, I do not like it:
Traditions please me best; I am not so precise,
To change true rules for odd inventions.

Miss, your father requests that you leave your books,
And help decorate your sister's room:
You know tomorrow is the wedding-day.

Farewell, both good teachers: I must go.

By my faith, mistress, then I have no reason to stay.

But I have reason to examine this teacher:
I think he looks like he is in love.
Yet if your thoughts, Bianca, are so without pride
To have feelings for every common person,
Stop such behavior: if I once find you ranging,
Hortensio will be done with you by changing.

Scene II

The same. Before BAPTISTA'S house

The same. In front of BAPTISTA'S house

[Enter BAPTISTA, GREMIO, TRANIO, KATHERINA, BIANCA, LUCENTIO, and ATTENDANTS.]

BAPTISTA.
[To TRANIO.]
Signior Lucentio, this is the 'pointed day
That Katherine and Petruchio should be married,
And yet we hear not of our son-in-law.
What will be said? What mockery will it be
To want the bridegroom when the priest attends

To speak the ceremonial rites of marriage!
What says Lucentio to this shame of ours?

Sir Lucentio, this is the appointed day
That Katherine and Petruchio should be married,
And yet I hear nothing of my son-in-law.
What will people say? How ridiculous it will be
To be without the bridegroom when the priest
attends
To speak the ceremonial rituals of marraige!
What does Lucentio say to this shame of mine?

KATHERINA.
No shame but mine; I must, forsooth, be forc'd
To give my hand, oppos'd against my heart,
Unto a mad-brain rudesby, full of spleen;
Who woo'd in haste and means to wed at leisure.

I told you, I, he was a frantic fool,
Hiding his bitter jests in blunt behaviour;
And to be noted for a merry man,
He'll woo a thousand, 'point the day of marriage,

Make friends invited, and proclaim the banns;
Yet never means to wed where he hath woo'd.
Now must the world point at poor Katherine,
And say 'Lo! there is mad Petruchio's wife,
If it would please him come and marry her.'

No shame but mine; I must, truthfully, be forced
To give my hand, opposed against my heart,
To a crazy rude man, full of arrogance;
Who wooed quickly and means to wed whenever
he feels like it.
I told you, I did, that he was a hasty fool,
Hiding his bitter jokes in blunt behavior;
And to be known as a cheerful man,
He'll woo a thousand, appoint the day of
marriage,
Invite friends, and announce the date;
Yet never means to wed where he has wooed.
Now the world must point at poor Katherine,
And say, 'Look! There is crazy Petruchio's wife,
If it would please him to come and marry her.'

TRANIO.
Patience, good Katherine, and Baptista too.
Upon my life, Petruchio means but well,
Whatever fortune stays him from his word:

Though he be blunt, I know him passing wise;
Though he be merry, yet withal he's honest.

Patience, good Katherine, and Baptista too.
By my life, Petruchio only means well,
Whatever fate is preventing him from fulfilling his
promise:
Though he is blunt, I know he is very wise;
Though he can be silly, he's always honest.

KATHERINA.
Would Katherine had never seen him though!

If only Katherine had never seen him though!

[Exit, weeping, followed by BIANCA and others.]

BAPTISTA.

Go, girl, I cannot blame thee now to weep,
For such an injury would vex a very saint;
Much more a shrew of thy impatient humour.

[Enter BIONDELLO.]

Master, master! News!
old news, and such news as you never heard of!

BAPTISTA.
Is it new and old too? How may that be?

BIONDELLO.
Why, is it not news to hear of Petruchio's coming?

BAPTISTA.
Is he come?

BIONDELLO.
Why, no, sir.

BAPTISTA.
What then?

BIONDELLO.
He is coming.

BAPTISTA.
When will he be here?

BIONDELLO.
When he stands where I am and sees you there.

TRANIO.
But, say, what to thine old news?

BIONDELLO.
Why, Petruchio is coming, in a new hat and an old
jerkin; a pair of old breeches thrice turned; a pair of
boots that have been candle-cases, one buckled,
another laced; an old rusty sword ta'en out of the town
armoury, with a broken hilt, and chapeless; with two
broken points: his horse hipped with an old mothy
saddle and stirrups of no kindred; besides, possessed
with the glanders and like to mose in the chine;
troubled with the lampass, infected with the fashions,
full of windgalls, sped with spavins, rayed with the
yellows, past cure of the fives, stark spoiled with the
staggers, begnawn with the bots, swayed in the back
and shoulder-shotten; near-legged before,

Go, girl, I cannot blame you for crying,
For such an offense would trouble a saint;
Even more so a rude woman of your impatient
personality.

Master, master! News!
old news, and such news as you never heard of!

Is it new and old too? How may that be?

Why, is it not news to hear of Petruchio's coming?

Is he come?

Why, no, sir.

What then?

He is coming.

When will he be here?

When he stands where I am and sees you there.

But, say, what is your old news?

Why, Petruchio is coming, in
[an extremely ragged and shabby outfit,
described in extreme but unimportant detail].

and with a half-checked bit, and a head-stall of sheep's
leather, which, being restrained to keep him from
stumbling, hath been often burst, and now repaired with
knots; one girth six times pieced, and a woman's crupper
of velure, which hath two letters for her name fairly set
down in studs, and here and there pieced with
pack-thread.

BAPTISTA.
Who comes with him?

Who comes with him?

BIONDELLO.
O, sir! his lackey, for all the world caparisoned like the
horse; with a linen stock on one leg and a kersey
boot-hose on the other, gartered with a red and blue
list; an old hat, and the 'humour of forty fancies' prick'd
in't for a feather: a monster, a very monster in apparel,
and not like a Christian footboy or a gentleman's
lackey.

Oh, sir, his servant, for all the world dressed like
the horse; [in also a terrible and embarrassing
outfit].

TRANIO.
'Tis some odd humour pricks him to this fashion;

Yet oftentimes lie goes but mean-apparell'd.

It is only some strange mood that makes him
behave like this;
Often he goes about in a poor man's clothes.

BAPTISTA.
I am glad he's come, howsoe'er he comes.

I am glad he has come, no matter how he comes.

BIONDELLO.
Why, sir, he comes not.

Why, sir, he does not come.

BAPTISTA.
Didst thou not say he comes?

Didn't you say he comes?

BIONDELLO.
Who? that Petruchio came?

Who? that Petruchio came?

BAPTISTA.
Ay, that Petruchio came.

Yes, that Petruchio came.

BIONDELLO.
No, sir; I say his horse comes, with him on his back.

No, sir; I say his horse comes, with him on his
back.

BAPTISTA.
Why, that's all one.

Why, that's all the same thing.

BIONDELLO.
Nay, by Saint Jamy,
I hold you a penny,
A horse and a man

No, by Saint Jamy,
I would bet you a penny,
A horse and a man

Is more than one,
And yet not many.

Is more than one,
And yet not many.

[Enter PETRUCHIO and GRUMIO.]

PETRUCHIO.
Come, where be these gallants? Who is at home?

Come, where are these young men? Who is at home?

BAPTISTA.
You are welcome, sir.

You are welcome, sir.

PETRUCHIO.
And yet I come not well.

And yet I do not come well.

BAPTISTA.
And yet you halt not.

And yet you do not hesitate.

TRANIO.
Not so well apparell'd
As I wish you were.

Not so well dressed
As I wish you were.

PETRUCHIO.
Were it better, I should rush in thus.
But where is Kate? Where is my lovely bride?
How does my father? Gentles, methinks you frown;

And wherefore gaze this goodly company,
As if they saw some wondrous monument,
Some comet or unusual prodigy?

If it was better, I would rush in this way.
But where is Kate? Where is my lovely bride?
How is my father? Gentleman, I think you are frowning;
And why is this good company staring,
As if they saw some startling sight,
Some comet or unusual happening?

BAPTISTA.
Why, sir, you know this is your wedding-day:
Now sadder, that you come so unprovided.
Fie! doff this habit, shame to your estate,

An eye-sore to our solemn festival.

First were we sad, fearing you would not come;
Now sadder, that you come looking so awful.
Enough! Take off these clothes, a shame to your wealth,
An eye-sore to our solemn festival.

TRANIO.
And tell us what occasion of import
Hath all so long detain'd you from your wife,
And sent you hither so unlike yourself?

And tell us what important thing
Has kept you from your wife for so long,
And sent you here so unlike yourself?

PETRUCHIO.
Tedious it were to tell, and harsh to hear;
Sufficeth, I am come to keep my word,

Though in some part enforced to digress;
Which at more leisure I will so excuse
As you shall well be satisfied withal.
But where is Kate? I stay too long from her;

It would be boring to tell, and harsh to hear;
Let it be enough to say that I have come to keep my word,
Though I was forced to not come straight away;
Which when I have more time I will explain
In such a way that you will be satisfied.
But where is Kate? I stay too long from her;

The morning wears, 'tis time we were at church.

TRANIO.
See not your bride in these unreverent robes;
Go to my chamber, put on clothes of mine.

PETRUCHIO.
Not I, believe me: thus I'll visit her.

BAPTISTA.
But thus, I trust, you will not marry her.

PETRUCHIO.
Good sooth, even thus; therefore ha' done with words;

To me she's married, not unto my clothes.
Could I repair what she will wear in me
As I can change these poor accoutrements,
'Twere well for Kate and better for myself.

But what a fool am I to chat with you
When I should bid good-morrow to my bride,
And seal the title with a lovely kiss!

[Exeunt PETRUCHIO, GRUMIO, and BIODELLO.]

TRANIO.
He hath some meaning in his mad attire.
We will persuade him, be it possible,
To put on better ere he go to church.

BAPTISTA.
I'll after him and see the event of this.

[Exeunt BAPTISTA, GREMIO and ATTENDENTS.]

TRANIO.
But to her love concerneth us to add
Her father's liking; which to bring to pass,
As I before imparted to your worship,
I am to get a man,--whate'er he be
It skills not much; we'll fit him to our turn,--

And he shall be Vincentio of Pisa,
And make assurance here in Padua,
Of greater sums than I have promised.

So shall you quietly enjoy your hope,
And marry sweet Bianca with consent.

The morning is passing by, it is time we were at church.

Do not see your bride in these inappropriate robes; Go to my room, put on clothes of mine.

Not I, believe me: I'll visit her like this.

But I trust you will not marry her like this.

Truthfully, just like this; therefore enough talking about it;
She's marrying me, not my clothes
If I could fix up what she will find in me
As I can change these shabby clothes,
It would be good for Kate and even better for myself.
But what a fool I am being to chat with you
When I should wish good morning to my bride,
And confirm the title with a lovely kiss!

He has some meaning in his crazy clothing.
We will convince him, if it is possible,
To put on better before he goes to church.

I'll go after him and see what follows.

But to her love it concerns us to add
Her father's liking; which to make happen,
As I previously told your worship,
I am to get a man, -- whoever he is
It doesn't really matter; we'll make him suit our needs, --
And he shall be Vincentio of Pisa,
And promise here in Padua
Even larger amounts of money than I have promised.
So you shall quietly get what you want,
And marry sweet Bianca with consent.

LUCENTIO.
Were it not that my fellow schoolmaster
Doth watch Bianca's steps so narrowly,
'Twere good, methinks, to steal our marriage;
Which once perform'd, let all the world say no,
I'll keep mine own despite of all the world.

If it were not that my fellow teacher
Watches Bianca's every move so carefully,
It would be good, I think, to elope;
Which once performed, let all the world say no,
I'll keep what is mine no matter what the world
says.

TRANIO.
That by degrees we mean to look into,
And watch our vantage in this business.
We'll over-reach the greybeard, Gremio,
The narrow-prying father, Minola,
The quaint musician, amorous Licio;
All for my master's sake, Lucentio.

We can plan to look into that bit by bit,
And watch our advantage in this business.
We'll outdo the old man, Gremio,
The careful father, Minola,
The quaint musician, passionate Licio;
All for my master's sake, Lucentio.

[Re-enter GREMIO.]

Signior Gremio, came you from the church?

Sir Gremio, did you come from the church?

GREMIO.
As willingly as e'er I came from school.

As willingly as I ever came from school.

TRANIO.
And is the bride and bridegroom coming home?

And is the bride and bridegroom coming home?

GREMIO.
A bridegroom, say you? 'Tis a groom indeed,
A grumbling groom, and that the girl shall find.

A bridegroom, you say? It is a groom indeed,
A grumbling groom, and that the girl shall find.

TRANIO.
Curster than she? Why, 'tis impossible.

More cursed than she is? Why, it's impossible.

GREMIO.
Why, he's a devil, a devil, a very fiend.

Why, he's a devil, a devil, a very fiend.

TRANIO.
Why, she's a devil, a devil, the devil's dam.

Why, she's a devil, a devil, the devil's wife.

GREMIO.
Tut! she's a lamb, a dove, a fool, to him.
I'll tell you, Sir Lucentio: when the priest
Should ask if Katherine should be his wife,
'Ay, by gogs-wouns' quoth he, and swore so loud
That, all amaz'd, the priest let fall the book;

And as he stoop'd again to take it up,
The mad-brain'd bridegroom took him such a cuff
That down fell priest and book, and book and priest:
'Now take them up,' quoth he 'if any list.'

Huh! She's a lamb, a dove, a fool - to him.
I'll tell you, Sir Lucentio: when the priest
Should ask if Katherine should be his wife,
'Yes, by God's wounds,' he says, and swore so loud
That, full of amazement, the priest dropped the
book;
And as he stooped again to pick it up,
The insane bridegroom gave him such a punch
That the priest and the book fell:
'Now pick them up,' he said, 'if any tilt.'

TRANIO.
What said the wench, when he rose again?

What did the girl say, when he rose again?

GREMIO.
Trembled and shook, for why, he stamp'd and swore

Trembled and shook, for why, he stamped and
swore

As if the vicar meant to cozen him.
But after many ceremonies done,
He calls for wine: 'A health!' quoth he, as if
He had been abroad, carousing to his mates

As if the vicar meant to cheat him.
But after the many ceremonies were finished,
He calls for wine: 'A health!' he says, as if
He had been out and about, having fun with his
friends

After a storm; quaff'd off the muscadel,
And threw the sops all in the sexton's face,
Having no other reason
But that his beard grew thin and hungerly
And seem'd to ask him sops as he was drinking.

After a storm; drank deeply out of his cup,
And threw what was left in the sexton's face,
Having no other reason
Except his beard became thin and hungry
And seemed to ask him for leftovers as was
drinking.

This done, he took the bride about the neck,
And kiss'd her lips with such a clamorous smack
That at the parting all the church did echo.

This done, he grabbed the bride around the neck,
And kissed her lips with such a loud smack
That when they separated the whole church
echoed.

And I, seeing this, came thence for very shame;
And after me, I know, the rout is coming.

And I, seeing this, came here out of shame;
And after me, I know, the turning of the tables is
coming.

Such a mad marriage never was before.
Hark, hark! I hear the minstrels play.

There was never such an insane marriage before.
Listen, listen! I hear the minstrels play.

[Music.]

[Enter PETRUCHIO, KATHERINA, BIANCA, BAPTISTA, HORTENSIO, GRUMIO, and Train.]

PETRUCHIO.
Gentlemen and friends, I thank you for your pains:

Gentlemen and friends, I thank you for your
troubles:

I know you think to dine with me to-day,
And have prepar'd great store of wedding cheer

I know you think to have dinner with me today,
And have prepared a huge feast of wedding
celebration

But so it is- my haste doth call me hence,

But this is the situation - my business means I must
go,

And therefore here I mean to take my leave.

And therefore I mean to leave from here.

BAPTISTA.
Is't possible you will away to-night?

Is it possible you will go away tonight?

PETRUCHIO.
I must away to-day before night come.
Make it no wonder: if you knew my business,
You would entreat me rather go than stay.
And, honest company, I thank you all,
That have beheld me give away myself

I must go away today before night comes.
Do not be surprised: if you knew my business,
You would beg me to go rather than stay.
And, honest company, I thank you all,
That have watched me give myself away

To this most patient, sweet, and virtuous wife.
Dine with my father, drink a health to me.
For I must hence; and farewell to you all.

TRANIO.
Let us entreat you stay till after dinner.

PETRUCHIO.
It may not be.

GREMIO.
Let me entreat you.

PETRUCHIO.
It cannot be.

KATHERINA.
Let me entreat you.

PETRUCHIO.
I am content.

KATHERINA.
Are you content to stay?

PETRUCHIO.
I am content you shall entreat me stay;
But yet not stay, entreat me how you can.

KATHERINA.
Now, if you love me, stay.

PETRUCHIO.
Grumio, my horse!

GRUMIO.
Ay, sir, they be ready; the oats have eaten the horses.

KATHERINA.
Nay, then,
Do what thou canst, I will not go to-day;
No, nor to-morrow, not till I please myself.
The door is open, sir; there lies your way;
You may be jogging whiles your boots are green;
For me, I'll not be gone till I please myself.
'Tis like you'll prove a jolly surly groom
That take it on you at the first so roundly.

PETRUCHIO.
O Kate! content thee: prithee be not angry.

To this most patient, sweet, and virtuous wife.
Dine with my father, drink a health to me.
For I must go from here; and farewell to you all.

Let us beg you to stay until after dinner.

It may not be.

Let me entreat you.

It cannot be.

Let me entreat you.

I am content.

Are you content to stay?

I am content you shall entreat me stay;
But yet not stay, entreat me how you can.

Now, if you love me, stay.

Grumio, my horse!

Ay, sir, they be ready; the oats have eaten the horses.

No, then,
Do what you can, I will not go today;
No, nor tomorrow, not until I please myself.
The door is open, sir; there lies your way;
You may run around while your boots are new;
For me, I will not go until I wish.
It is likely you'll turn out to be a grumpy groom
That acts like this from the very first.

Oh Kate! Be content: please do not be angry.

KATHERINA.
I will be angry: what hast thou to do?
Father, be quiet; he shall stay my leisure.

I will be angry: what can you do about it?
Father, be quiet; he shall stay at my convenience.

GREMIO.
Ay, marry, sir, now it begins to work.

Yes, by Mary, sir, it's starting.

KATHERINA.
Gentlemen, forward to the bridal dinner:
I see a woman may be made a fool,
If she had not a spirit to resist.

Gentleman, let us go forward to the bridal dinner:
I see a woman may be made a fool,
If she does not have the spirit to resist.

PETRUCHIO.
They shall go forward, Kate, at thy command.
Obey the bride, you that attend on her;
Go to the feast, revel and domineer,
Carouse full measure to her maidenhead,
Be mad and merry, or go hang yourselves:
But for my bonny Kate, she must with me.
Nay, look not big, nor stamp, nor stare, nor fret;
I will be master of what is mine own.
She is my goods, my chattels; she is my house,
My household stuff, my field, my barn,
My horse, my ox, my ass, my anything;
And here she stands, touch her whoever dare;

I'll bring mine action on the proudest he
That stops my way in Padua. Grumio,
Draw forth thy weapon; we are beset with thieves;
Rescue thy mistress, if thou be a man.
Fear not, sweet wench; they shall not touch thee, Kate;

I'll buckler thee against a million.

They shall go forward, Kate, at your command.
Obey the bride, you that serve her;
Go the feast, revel and enjoy,
Celebrate her new married status,
Be wild and cheery, or go hang yourselves:
But for my pretty Kate, she must go with me.
No, don't pout, or stamp, or glare, or fuss;
I will be master of what is mine.
She is my property; she is my house,
My household stuff, my field, my barn,
My horse, my ox, my ass, my anything;
And here she stands, and whoever dares touch her;
I'll take action against the proudest man
That blocks my way in Padua. Grumio,
Draw your weapon; we are attacked by thieves;
Rescue your lady, if you are a man.
Do not fear, sweet girl; they will not touch you, Kate;
I would guard you against a million.

[Exeunt PETRUCHIO, KATHERINA, and GRUMIO.]

BAPTISTA.
Nay, let them go, a couple of quiet ones.

No, let them go, a pair of quiet ones.

GREMIO.
Went they not quickly, I should die with laughing.

If they did not go quickly, I would die of laughing.

TRANIO.
Of all mad matches, never was the like.

Of all insane matches, I never saw one like it.

LUCENTIO.
Mistress, what's your opinion of your sister?

Miss, what's your opinion of your sister?

BIANCA.
That, being mad herself, she's madly mated.

That, being mad herself, she's madly mated.

GREMIO.
I warrant him, Petruchio is Kated.

BAPTISTA.
Neighbours and friends, though bride and bridegroom wants
For to supply the places at the table,
You know there wants no junkets at the feast.

Lucentio, you shall supply the bridegroom's place;
And let Bianca take her sister's room.

TRANIO.
Shall sweet Bianca practise how to bride it?

BAPTISTA.
She shall, Lucentio. Come, gentlemen, let's go.

[Exeunt.]

I warrant him, Petruchio is Kated.

Neighbors and friends, though we lack the bride and bridegroom
To supply the places at the table,
You know there is no lack of anything else at the feast.
Lucentio, you shall fill the bridegroom's place;
And let Bianca take her sister's place.

Will sweet Bianca practice playing a bride?

She shall, Lucentio. Come, gentlemen, let's go.

Act IV

Scene I

A hall in PETRUCHIO'S country house

[Enter GRUMIO.]

GRUMIO.
Fie, fie on all tired jades, on all mad masters, and all foul ways! Was ever man so beaten? Was ever man so ray'd? Was ever man so weary? I am sent before to make a fire, and they are coming after to warm them. Now, were not I a little pot and soon hot, my very lips might freeze to my teeth, my tongue to the roof of my mouth, my heart in my belly, ere I should come by a fire to thaw me. But I with blowing the fire shall warm myself; for, considering the weather, a taller man than I will take cold. Holla, ho! Curtis!

Enough, enough with all tired servants, and all insane masters, and all terrible ways! Was any other man ever so beaten? Was any other man ever so worn out? Was any other man ever so exhausted? I have been sent before them to make a fire, and they are coming after to warm themselves. Now, if I were not a little man and soon warmed, my actual lips might freeze to my teeth, my tongue to the roof of my mouth, my heart in my belly, before I came to a fire to thaw. But I shall warm myself with blowing the fire; for, considering the weather, a taller man than I will catch a cold. Hello! Curtis!

[Enter CURTIS.]

CURTIS.
Who is that calls so coldly?

Who is that calls so coldly?

GRUMIO.
A piece of ice: if thou doubt it, thou mayst slide from my shoulder to my heel with no greater a run but my head and my neck. A fire, good Curtis.

A piece of ice; if you doubt it, you may slide from my shoulder to my heel with no greater friction than that made by my head and my neck. A fire, good Curtis.

CURTIS.
Is my master and his wife coming, Grumio?

Is my master and his wife coming, Grumio?

GRUMIO.
O, ay! Curtis, ay;
and therefore fire, fire; cast on no water.

*Oh, yes! Curtis, yes;
and therefore fire, fire; do not pour on any water.*

CURTIS.
Is she so hot a shrew as she's reported?

Is she as unpleasant a woman as they say?

GRUMIO.
She was, good Curtis, before this frost; but thou knowest winter tames man, woman, and beast; for it hath tamed my old master, and my new mistress, and myself, fellow Curtis.

She was, good Curtis, before this frost; but you know winter tames man, woman, and beast; for it has tamed my old master, and my new lady, and myself, fellow Curtis.

CURTIS.
Away, you three-inch fool! I am no beast

Away, you three-inch fool! I am no beast

GRUMIO.
Am I but three inches? Why, thy horn is a foot;
and so long am I at the least. But wilt thou make a fire,
or shall I complain on thee to our mistress, whose hand,
--she being now at hand,-- thou shalt soon feel, to thy
cold comfort, for being slow in thy hot office?

CURTIS.
I prithee, good Grumio, tell me, how goes the world?

GRUMIO.
A cold world, Curtis, in every office but thine;
and therefore fire. Do thy duty, and have thy duty,
for my master and mistress are almost frozen to death.

CURTIS.
There's fire ready; and therefore, good Grumio,
the news?

GRUMIO.
Why, 'Jack boy! ho, boy!"
and as much news as thou wilt.'

CURTIS.
Come, you are so full of cony-catching.

GRUMIO.
Why, therefore, fire; for I have caught extreme cold.
Where's the cook? Is supper ready, the house trimmed,
rushes strewed, cobwebs swept, the serving-men in
their new fustian, their white stockings, and every
officer his wedding-garment on? Be the Jacks fair
within, the Jills fair without, and carpets laid, and
everything in order?

CURTIS.
All ready; and therefore, I pray thee, news?

GRUMIO.
First, know my horse is tired;
my master and mistress fallen out.

CURTIS.
How?

GRUMIO.
Out of their saddles into the dirt;
and thereby hangs a tale.

CURTIS.

Am I only three inches? Why, your horn is a foot; and I am at least that long. But will you make a fire, or shall I complain about you to our lady, whose hand, -- since she is now at hand, -- you shall soon feel, to your cold comfort, for being slow at your hot job?

Please tell me, good Grumio, how is the world going?

A cold world, Curtis, in every position except yours; and therefore fire. Do your duty, and have your duty, for my master and lady are almost frozen to death.

There's fire ready; and therefore, good Grumio, the news?

Why, 'Jack boy! ho, boy!' and as much news as you want.

Come, you are so full of rabbit-catching [teasing].

Why, therefore, fire; for I have caught extreme cold. Where's the cook? Is supper ready, the house decorated, floor tidy, cobwebs swept, the serving-men in their new suits, their white stockings, and every officer wearing his wedding-clothes? Are the men neat inside, the women neat outside, and carpets rolled out, and everything in order?

All ready; and therefore, please tell me, news?

First, know my horse is tired; my master and mistress fallen out.

How?

Out of their saddles into the dirt; and there is a story behind that.

Let's ha't, good Grumio.

GRUMIO.
Lend thine ear.

CURTIS.
Here.

GRUMIO.
[Striking him.] There.

CURTIS.
This 'tis to feel a tale, not to hear a tale.

GRUMIO.
And therefore 'tis called a sensible tale; and this cuff
was but to knock at your car and beseech listening.
Now I begin: Imprimis, we came down a foul hill,
my master riding behind my mistress,--

CURTIS.
Both of one horse?

GRUMIO.
What's that to thee?

CURTIS.
Why, a horse.

GRUMIO.
Tell thou the tale: but hadst thou not crossed me,
thou shouldst have heard how her horse fell and she
under her horse; thou shouldst have heard in how
miry a place, how she was bemoiled; how he left her
with the horse upon her; how he beat me because
her horse stumbled; how she waded through the dirt
to pluck him off me: how he swore; how she prayed,
that never prayed before; how I cried; how the horses
ran away; how her bridle was burst; how I lost my
crupper; with many things of worthy memory,
which now shall die in oblivion, and thou return
unexperienced to thy grave.

CURTIS.
By this reckoning he is more shrew than she.

GRUMIO.
Ay; and that thou and the proudest of you all shall
find when he comes home. But what talk I of this?

Let's have it, good Grumio.

Lend your ear.

Here.

[Hitting him.] There.

That's to feel a story, not to hear a story.

*And therefore it's called a sensible story; and this
slap was just to make you stop being irritating.
Now I begin: to start with, we came down an awful
hill, my master riding behind my lady, --*

Both on one horse?

What's it to you?

*You tell the story then: but if you had not irritated
me, you would have heard about how her horse
fell and she under her horse; you would have
heard how muddy it was, how she was soiled; how
he left her with the horse on top of her; how he
beat me because her horse stumbled; how she
waded through the dirt to pull him off me: how he
swore; how she prayed, she who never prayed
before; how I cried; how the horses ran away;
how her bridle tore; how I lost my shoe; with
many things worth remembering, which shall now
die unknown, and you return inexperienced to
your grave.*

By this account he is more unbearable than she is.

*Yes; and you along with the best of you all will
discover that when he comes home. But why am I
still talking?*

Call forth Nathaniel, Joseph, Nicholas, Philip, Walter, Sugarsop, and the rest; let their heads be sleekly combed, their blue coats brush'd and their garters of an indifferent knit; let them curtsy with their left legs, and not presume to touch a hair of my master's horse-tail till they kiss their hands. Are they all ready?

Call Nathaniel, Joseph, Nicholas, Philip, Walter, Sugarsop, and the rest; let their heads be smoothly combed, their blue coats brushed and their garters matching; let them bow with their left legs, and not dare to touch a hair of my master's horse-tail until they kiss their hands. Are they all ready?

CURTIS.
They are.

They are.

GRUMIO.
Call them forth.

Call them to come here.

CURTIS.
Do you hear? ho!
You must meet my master to countenance my mistress.

Do you hear? Hey!
You must meet my master and countenance [get to know] my lady.

GRUMIO.
Why, she hath a face of her own.

Why, she has a face [another meaning of 'countenance'] of her own.

CURTIS.
Who knows not that?

Who doesn't know that?

GRUMIO.
Thou, it seems,
that calls for company to countenance her.

You, it seems,
that calls for company to 'countenance' her.

CURTIS.
I call them forth to credit her.

I mean I want them to give her credit.

GRUMIO.
Why, she comes to borrow nothing of them.

Why, she's not borrowing anything from them [he's thinking of 'credit' as in money].

[Enter several SERVANTS.]

NATHANIEL.
Welcome home, Grumio!

Welcome home, Grumio!

PHILIP.
How now, Grumio!

What's going on, Grumio?

JOSEPH.
What, Grumio!

What, Grumio!

NICHOLAS.
Fellow Grumio!

Fellow Grumio!

NATHANIEL.
How now, old lad!

How are things, old man?

GRUMIO.
Welcome, you; how now, you; what, you; fellow,
you; and thus much for greeting. Now, my spruce
companions, is all ready, and all things neat?

Welcome, you; what's going on, you; what, you;
fellow, you; and so much for my greetings. Now,
my well-groomed companions, is all ready, and all
things neat?

NATHANIEL.
All things is ready. How near is our master?

Everything's ready. How near is our master?

GRUMIO.
E'en at hand, alighted by this; and therefore be not,
-- Cock's passion, silence! I hear my master.

Almost here; and therefore do not be, --
My goodness, silence! I hear my master.

[Enter PETRUCHIO and KATHERINA.]

PETRUCHIO.
Where be these knaves?
What! no man at door
To hold my stirrup nor to take my horse?
Where is Nathaniel, Gregory, Philip?--

Where are these rascals?
What?! No mat at the door
To hold my stirrup nor to take my horse?
Where is Nathaniel, Gregory, Philip?--

ALL SERVANTS.
Here, here, sir; here, sir.

Here, here, sir; here, sir.

PETRUCHIO.
Here, sir! here, sir! here, sir! here, sir!
You logger-headed and unpolish'd grooms!
What, no attendance? no regard? no duty?
Where is the foolish knave I sent before?

Here, sir! here, sir! here, sir! here, sir!
You softheaded and incapable grooms!
What, no service? no respect? no duty?
Where is the foolish rascal I sent before me?

GRUMIO.
Here, sir; as foolish as I was before.

Here, sir; as foolish as I was before.

PETRUCHIO.
You peasant swain! you whoreson malt-horse drudge!

Did I not bid thee meet me in the park,
And bring along these rascal knaves with thee?

You peasant child! You son of a prostitute, lowly
servant!
Did I not order you to meet me outside,
And bring along these rascals with you?

GRUMIO.
Nathaniel's coat, sir, was not fully made,
And Gabriel's pumps were all unpink'd i' the heel;
There was no link to colour Peter's hat,
And Walter's dagger was not come from sheathing;
There was none fine but Adam, Ralph, and Gregory;

The rest were ragged, old, and beggarly;

Yet, as they are, here are they come to meet you.

Nathaniel's coat, sir, was not finished,
And Gabriel's shoes were all worn at the heel;
Peter's hat was lacking in color,
And Walter's dagger was stuck in its sheath;
None of them looked good except Adam, Ralph,
and Gregory;
The rest were ragged, old, and looked like
beggars;
Yet, as they are, here they have come to meet you.

PETRUCHIO.

Go, rascals, go and fetch my supper in.

[Exeunt some of the SERVANTS.]

Where is the life that late I led? Where are those--?

Sit down, Kate, and welcome. Soud, soud, soud, soud!

[Re-enter SERVANTS with supper.]

Why, when, I say?
--Nay, good sweet Kate, be merry.--
Off with my boots, you rogues! you villains! when?
It was the friar of orders grey,
As he forth walked on his way:
Out, you rogue! you pluck my foot awry:

[Strikes him.]

Take that, and mend the plucking off the other.
Be merry, Kate. Some water, here; what, ho!
Where's my spaniel Troilus?
Sirrah, get you hence
And bid my cousin Ferdinand come hither:

[Exit SERVANT.]

One, Kate, that you must kiss and be acquainted with.

Where are my slippers?
Shall I have some water?
Come, Kate, and wash, and welcome heartily.--

[SERVANT lets the ewer fall. PETRUCHIO strikes him.]

You whoreson villain! will you let it fall?

KATHERINA.
Patience, I pray you; 'twas a fault unwilling.

PETRUCHIO.
A whoreson, beetle-headed, flap-ear'd knave!
[A series of insults.]
Come, Kate, sit down; I know you have a stomach.
Will you give thanks, sweet Kate, or else shall I?--
--What's this? Mutton?

FIRST SERVANT.
Ay.

Go, rascals, go and get my supper and bring it.

Where is the life that I used to lead? Where are those --?
Sit down, Kate, and welcome. Come on, come on, come on, come on!

Why, when, I say?
--No, good sweet Kate, be cheerful.--
Take off my boots, you rogues! you villains! when?
It was a friar dressed in gray,
As he walked off upon his way:
Out, you rogue! You hurt my foot when you tugged:

Take that, and do a better job pulling off the other.
Cheer up, Kate. Some water here; hey!
Where's my dog Troilus?
You, get yourself away
And tell my cousin Ferdinand to come here:

One, Kate, that you must kiss and be acquainted with.
Where are my slippers?
Shall I have some water?
Come, Kate, and wash, and welcome heartily.--

[SERVANT drops the jug. PETRUCHIO hits him.]

You son of a prostitute! Will you let it fall?

Patience, I beg you; it was an accident.

A whoreson, beetle-headed, flap-ear'd knave!

Come, Kate, sit down; I know you are hungry.
Will you say grace, sweet Kate, or shall I instead?
--What's this? Mutton?

Yes.

PETRUCHIO.
Who brought it?

Who brought it?

PETER.
I.

I.

PETRUCHIO.
'Tis burnt; and so is all the meat.
What dogs are these! Where is the rascal cook?

How durst you, villains, bring it from the dresser,
And serve it thus to me that love it not?

It's burnt; and so is all the food.
What dogs these people are! Where is the rascal cook?
How dare you, villains, bring it from the kitchen,
And serve it like this to me that hates it?

[Throws the meat, etc., at them.]

There, take it to you, trenchers, cups, and all.
You heedless joltheads and unmanner'd slaves!
What! do you grumble? I'll be with you straight.

There, take it to you, plates, cups, and all.
You heedless joltheads and unmanner'd slaves!
What! Do you complain? I'll show you.

KATHERINA.
I pray you, husband, be not so disquiet;
The meat was well, if you were so contented.

I beg you, husband, do not be so upset;
The meat was all right, if you would put up with it.

PETRUCHIO.
I tell thee, Kate, 'twas burnt and dried away,
And I expressly am forbid to touch it;
For it engenders choler, planteth anger;
And better 'twere that both of us did fast,

Since, of ourselves, ourselves are choleric,
Than feed it with such over-roasted flesh.
Be patient; to-morrow 't shall be mended.
And for this night we'll fast for company:
Come, I will bring thee to thy bridal chamber.

I tell you, Kate, it was burnt and dried to nothing
And I am particularly forbidden to touch it
For it causes irritation, gives rise to anger;
And it would be better if both of us went without food,
Since, we ourselves are irritable people,
That feed it with such overly cooked meat.
Be patient; tomorrow it will be fixed.
And as for tonight we'll go without food together;
Come, I will take you to your bedroom.

[Exeunt PETRUCHIO, KATHERINA, and CURTIS.]

NATHANIEL.
Peter, didst ever see the like?

Peter, did you ever see anything like it?

PETER.
He kills her in her own humour.

He's beating her at her own game.

[Re-enter CURTIS.]

GRUMIO.
Where is he?

Where is he?

CURTIS.
In her chamber, making a sermon of continency to her;

In her room, preaching about self-restraint to her;

And rails, and swears, and rates, that she, poor soul,

Knows not which way to stand, to look, to speak,

And sits as one new risen from a dream.
Away, away! for he is coming hither.

[Exeunt.]

[Re-enter PETRUCHIO.]

PETRUCHIO.
Thus have I politicly begun my reign,
And 'tis my hope to end successfully.
My falcon now is sharp and passing empty.
And till she stoop she must not be full-gorg'd,

For then she never looks upon her lure.
Another way I have to man my haggard,
To make her come, and know her keeper's call,
That is, to watch her, as we watch these kites
That bate and beat, and will not be obedient.
She eat no meat to-day, nor none shall eat;
Last night she slept not, nor to-night she shall not;

As with the meat, some undeserved fault

I'll find about the making of the bed;
And here I'll fling the pillow, there the bolster,
This way the coverlet, another way the sheets;
Ay, and amid this hurly I intend
That all is done in reverend care of her;

And, in conclusion, she shall watch all night:
And if she chance to nod I'll rail and brawl,
And with the clamour keep her still awake.
This is a way to kill a wife with kindness;
And thus I'll curb her mad and headstrong humour.

He that knows better how to tame a shrew,
Now let him speak; 'tis charity to show.

[Exit.]

And yells, and swears, and stamps, so that she, poor soul,
Does not know which way to stand, to look, to speak,
And sits as one just awake from a dream.
Away, away! For he is coming here.

In this way I have strategically begun my rule,
And it's my hope to end successfully.
My falcon [Kate] is now very hungry.
And until she gives in she must not be full or comfortable.
For then she will never behave as I wish.
I have another way to train my wife,
To make her come, and know her keeper's call,
That is, to watch her, as we watch these hawks
That bite and fight, and will not be obedient.
She ate no food today, and she will eat none;
Last night she did not sleep, and tonight she shall not;
As with the food, I'll find some nonexistent problem
With the making of the bed;
And here I'll throw the pillow, there the comforter,
This way the covers, another way the sheets;
Yes, and among this chaos I will make it seem
That all this is because I want to take good care of her;
And, in conclusion, she shall be awake all night:
And if she starts to fall asleep I'll yell and holler,
And with the noise keep her awake still.
This is a way to kill a wife with kindness;
And this is how I will stop her crazy and stubborn ways,
He that has a better idea of how to tame a shrew,
Now let him speak; I would consider it a favor.

Scene II

Padua. Before BAPTISTA'S house

[Enter TRANIO and HORTENSIO.]

TRANIO.
Is 't possible, friend Licio, that Mistress Bianca
Doth fancy any other but Lucentio?
I tell you, sir, she bears me fair in hand.

*Is it possible, my friend Licio, that Miss Bianca
Has a fondness for anyone other than Lucentio?
I tell you, sir, she likes me very much.*

HORTENSIO.
Sir, to satisfy you in what I have said,
Stand by and mark the manner of his teaching.

*Sir, to see the proof of what I have said,
Stand by and watch the way he teaches.*

[They stand aside.]

[Enter BIANCA and LUCENTIO.]

LUCENTIO.
Now, mistress, profit you in what you read?

Now, miss, are you benefiting by what you read?

BIANCA.
What, master, read you,
First resolve me that.

*What, master, you read,
First resolve me that.*

LUCENTIO.
I read that I profess, the Art to Love.

I read what I feel, the Art to Love.

BIANCA.
And may you prove, sir, master of your art!

*And may you turn out, sir, to be master of your
art!*

LUCENTIO.
While you, sweet dear, prove mistress of my heart.

*While you, sweet dear, turn out to be the lady of
my heart.*

[They retire.]

HORTENSIO.
Quick proceeders, marry!
Now tell me, I pray,
You that durst swear that your Mistress Bianca
Lov'd none in the world so well as Lucentio.

*Fast-moving lovers, indeed!
Now tell me, please,
You that dared to swear that your Miss Bianca
Did not love anyone in the world as much as
Lucentio.*

TRANIO.
O despiteful love! unconstant womankind!
I tell thee, Licio, this is wonderful.

*Oh, spiteful love! Unfaithful womankind!
I tell you, Licio, this astonishes me.*

HORTENSIO.

Mistake no more; I am not Licio.
Nor a musician as I seem to be;
But one that scorn to live in this disguise
For such a one as leaves a gentleman
And makes a god of such a cullion:
Know, sir, that I am call'd Hortensio.

TRANIO.
Signior Hortensio, I have often heard
Of your entire affection to Bianca;
And since mine eyes are witness of her lightness,

I will with you, if you be so contented,
Forswear Bianca and her love for ever.

HORTENSIO.
See, how they kiss and court! Signior Lucentio,
Here is my hand, and here I firmly vow
Never to woo her more, but do forswear her,
As one unworthy all the former favours
That I have fondly flatter'd her withal.

TRANIO.
And here I take the like unfeigned oath,
Never to marry with her though she would entreat;
Fie on her! See how beastly she doth court him!

HORTENSIO.
Would all the world but he had quite forsworn!
For me, that I may surely keep mine oath,
I will be married to a wealtlly widow
Ere three days pass, which hath as long lov'd me

As I have lov'd this proud disdainful haggard.
And so farewell, Signior Lucentio.
Kindness in women, not their beauteous looks,

Shall win my love; and so I take my leave,
In resolution as I swore before.

[Exit HORTENSIO. LUCENTIO and BIANCA advance.]

TRANIO.
Mistress Bianca, bless you with such grace
As 'longeth to a lover's blessed case!
Nay, I have ta'en you napping, gentle love,
And have forsworn you with Hortensio.

BIANCA.

Make no mistake; I am not Licio.
Nor a musician as I seem to be;
But one that resents living in this disguise
For such a one as leaves a gentleman
And makes a god of such a lowly person;
Know, sir, that I am call'd Hortensio.

Sir Hortensio, I have often heard
Of your deep affection for Bianca;
And since my eyes have witnessed her
unfaithfulness,
I will with you, if you wish,
Give up Bianca and her love forever.

See, how they kiss and court! Signior Lucentio,
Here is my hand, and here I firmly promise
Never to woo her again, but give her up,
As one unworthy of all the former favors
That I had fondly flattered her with before.

And here I make the same not-faked promise,
Never to marry her even if she begged me;
Enough with her! See how terrible she is!

If only all the world except him had given her up!
For me, so I may surely keep my promise,
I will be married to a wealthy widow
Before three days pass, who has loved me for as
long
As I have loved this proud, stuck-up woman.
And so farewell, Signior Lucentio.
Kindness in women, not their beautiful
appearance,
Shall win my love; and so I will leave now,
Resolved as I promised before.

Miss Bianca, bless you with such luck
As belong to a lover's blessed case!
I have surprised you, gentle love,
And have given you up with Hortensio.

Tranio, you jest; but have you both forsworn me?

TRANIO.
Mistress, we have.

LUCENTIO.
Then we are rid of Licio.

TRANIO.
I' faith, he'll have a lusty widow now,
That shall be woo'd and wedded in a day.

BIANCA.
God give him joy!

TRANIO.
Ay, and he'll tame her.

BIANCA.
He says so, Tranio.

TRANIO.
Faith, he is gone unto the taming-school.

BIANCA.
The taming-school! What, is there such a place?

TRANIO.
Ay, mistress; and Petruchio is the master,
That teacheth tricks eleven and twenty long,
To tame a shrew and charm her chattering tongue.

[Enter BIONDELLO, running.]

BIONDELLO.
O master, master! I have watch'd so long
That I am dog-weary; but at last I spied
An ancient angel coming down the hill
Will serve the turn.

TRANIO.
What is he, Biondello?

BIONDELLO.
Master, a mercatante or a pedant,
I know not what; but formal in apparel,
In gait and countenance surely like a father.

LUCENTIO.

Tranio, you're kidding; but have you both given me up?

Mistress, we have.

Then we are rid of Licio.

*By my faith, he'll have an energetic widow now,
That shall be wooed and married in a day.*

God give him joy!

Yes, and he'll tame her.

He says so, Tranio.

Faith, he has gone to the taming-school.

The taming-school! What, is there such a place?

*Yes, miss; and Petruchio is the teacher,
That teaches many kinds of tricks,
To tame a shrew and calm her excessive chatter.*

*Oh master, master! I have watched so long
That I am exhausted; but at last I noticed
An elderly gentleman coming down the hill
Who will suit your need.*

What is he, Biondello?

*Master, a merchant or a traveling teacher,
I don't know what; but dressed formally,
In way of walking and appearance surely like a father.*

And what of him, Tranio?

TRANIO.
If he be credulous and trust my tale,
I'll make him glad to seem Vincentio,
And give assurance to Baptista Minola,
As if he were the right Vincentio.
Take in your love, and then let me alone.

[Exeunt LUCENTIO and BIANCA.]

[Enter a PEDANT.]

PEDANT.
God save you, sir!

TRANIO.
And you, sir! you are welcome.
Travel you far on, or are you at the farthest?

PEDANT.
Sir, at the farthest for a week or two;
But then up farther, and as far as Rome;
And so to Tripoli, if God lend me life.

TRANIO.
What countryman, I pray?

PEDANT.
Of Mantua.

TRANIO.
Of Mantua, sir? Marry, God forbid,
And come to Padua, careless of your life!

PEDANT.
My life, sir! How, I pray? for that goes hard.

TRANIO.
'Tis death for any one in Mantua
To come to Padua. Know you not the cause?
Your ships are stay'd at Venice; and the duke,
-- For private quarrel 'twixt your duke and him,--

Hath publish'd and proclaim'd it openly.
'Tis marvel, but that you are but newly come
You might have heard it else proclaim'd about.

PEDANT.
Alas, sir! it is worse for me than so;

And what about him, Tranio?

If he believes things easily and trusts my tale,
I'll make him glad to seem Vincentio,
And give assurance to Baptista Minola,
As if he were the actual Vincentio.
Take your love inside, and then leave me alone.

And you, sir! You are welcome.
Are you traveling much further, or is this your
destination?

Sir, this is as far as I'm going for a week or two;
But then up farther, and as far as Rome;
And so to Tripoli, if God lend me life.

What country are you from, may I ask?

Of Mantua.

You are of Mantua, sir? By Mary, God forbid,
And come to Padua, so recklessly with your life!

My life, sir! How, may I ask? For I would hate to
lose it.

It's certain death for anyone in Manua
To come to Padua. Don't you know why?
Your ships are stranded in Venice; and the duke,
-- Because of a private quarrel between your duke
and him, --
Has published and proclaimed it all around.
It is a marvel, and if you hadn't been so new here
You would have otherwise might have heard it
announced.

Oh no, sir! It will be even worse for me;

For I have bills for money by exchange
From Florence, and must here deliver them.

TRANIO.
Well, sir, to do you courtesy,
This will I do, and this I will advise you:
First, tell me, have you ever been at Pisa?

PEDANT.
Ay, sir, in Pisa have I often been,
Pisa renowned for grave citizens.

TRANIO.
Among them know you one Vincentio?

PEDANT.
I know him not, but I have heard of him,
A merchant of incomparable wealth.

TRANIO.
He is my father, sir; and, sooth to say,
In countenance somewhat doth resemble you.

BIONDELLO.
[Aside.]
As much as an apple doth an oyster, and all one.

TRANIO.
To save your life in this extremity,
This favour will I do you for his sake;
And think it not the worst of all your fortunes
That you are like to Sir Vincentio.
His name and credit shall you undertake,
And in my house you shall be friendly lodg'd;
Look that you take upon you as you should!
You understand me, sir; so shall you stay
Till you have done your business in the city.
If this be courtesy, sir, accept of it.

PEDANT.
O, sir, I do; and will repute you ever
The patron of my life and liberty.

TRANIO.
Then go with me to make the matter good.
This, by the way, I let you understand:
My father is here look'd for every day
To pass assurance of a dower in marriage
'Twixt me and one Baptista's daughter here:

For I have bills for money by exchange
From Florence, and must deliver them here.

Well, sir, to do you a favor,
I will do this, and I will give you this advice:
First, tell me, have you ever been to Pisa?

Yes, sir, I have often been to Pisa,
Pisa which is well known for its wise citizens.

Among them do you know Vincentio?

I do not know him, but I have heard of him,
A merchant of incomparable wealth.

He is my father, sir; and, to tell the truth,
Has a face that somewhat resembles yours.

As much as an apple looks like an oyster, anyway.

To save your life in this difficulty,
I will do you this favor for his sake;
And do not think it the worst of your luck
That you are similar to Sir Vincentio.
You shall take his name and duties,
And in my house you shall be lodged as a friend;
Make sure you behave as you should!
You understand me, sir; and so you shall stay
Till you have done your business in the city.
If this be courtesy, sir, accept of it.

Oh, sir, I do; and will always consider you
The savior of my life and liberty.

Then go with me to settle the matter.
This, by the way, I let you understand:
My father is waited for here every day
To promise a dower in marriage
Between me and a man named Baptista's
daughter, here;

In all these circumstances I'll instruct you.
Go with me to clothe you as becomes you.

[Exeunt.]

In all these circumstances I'll instruct you.
Go with me to clothe you as fits the role.

Scene III

A room in PETRUCHIO'S house

[Enter KATHERINA and GRUMIO.]

GRUMIO.
No, no, forsooth; I dare not for my life.

No, no, truthfully; I do not dare - it's life or death.

KATHERINA.
The more my wrong, the more his spite appears.

The more I am wronged, the more his anger appears.

What, did he marry me to famish me?
Beggars that come unto my father's door
Upon entreaty have a present alms;
If not, elsewhere they meet with charity;
But I, who never knew how to entreat,
Nor never needed that I should entreat,
Am starv'd for meat, giddy for lack of sleep;
With oaths kept waking, and with brawling fed.
And that which spites me more than all these wants,

What, did he marry me to starve me?
Beggars that come to my father's door
After begging receive a small donation;
And even if not, they get charity somewhere else;
But I, who never knew how to beg,
Or never needed to beg,
Am starved for food, dizzy for lack of sleep;
With yells kept awake, and with noise fed.
And that which bothers me more than all these wants,

He does it under name of perfect love;
As who should say, if I should sleep or eat
'Twere deadly sickness, or else present death.

He does it in the name of perfect love;
As if saying, if I slept or ate
That it were deadly sickness, or else immediate death.

I prithee go and get me some repast;
I care not what, so it be wholesome food.

Please go and get me a meal;
I do not care what, as long as it is nutritious food.

GRUMIO.
What say you to a neat's foot?

What would you say to a pig's foot?

KATHERINA.
'Tis passing good; I prithee let me have it.

That would be very good; please let me have it.

GRUMIO.
I fear it is too choleric a meat.
How say you to a fat tripe finely broil'd?

I fear it would be too rich for you.
What about some finely boiled tripe?

KATHERINA.
I like it well; good Grumio, fetch it me.

I like it very much; good Grumio, bring it to me.

GRUMIO.
I cannot tell; I fear 'tis choleric.
What say you to a piece of beef and mustard?

I can't tell; I fear it is too rich.
What do you say to a piece of beef and mustard?

KATHERINA.
A dish that I do love to feed upon.

A dish that I do love to eat.

GRUMIO.
Ay, but the mustard is too hot a little.

Yes, but the mustard is a little too hot.

KATHERINA.
Why then the beef, and let the mustard rest.

Why then the beef, and skip the mustard.

GRUMIO.
Nay, then I will not: you shall have the mustard,
Or else you get no beef of Grumio.

*No, then I will not; you shall have the mustard,
Or else you will get no beef from Grumio.*

KATHERINA.
Then both, or one, or anything thou wilt.

Then both, or one, or anything you wish.

GRUMIO.
Why then the mustard without the beef.

Why then the mustard without the beef.

KATHERINA.
Go, get thee gone, thou false deluding slave,

Get out of here, you lying slave,

[Beats him.]

That feed'st me with the very name of meat.
Sorrow on thee and all the pack of you

*That feeds me just the name of food.
May unhappiness come to you and all the rest of
the pack*

That triumph thus upon my misery!
Go, get thee gone, I say.

*That are enjoying my misery!
Go, get out of here, I say.*

[Enter PETRUCHIO with a dish of meat; and HORTENSIO.]

PETRUCHIO.
How fares my Kate? What, sweeting, all amort?

How is my Kate? All is well, sweeting?

HORTENSIO.
Mistress, what cheer?

How are you, madame?

KATHERINA.
Faith, as cold as can be.

Faith, as cold as can be.

PETRUCHIO.
Pluck up thy spirits; look cheerfully upon me.
Here, love; thou seest how diligent I am,
To dress thy meat myself, and bring it thee:

*Lift your spirits; look cheerfully on me.
Here, love; you see how hardworking I am,
To prepare your food myself, and bring it to you:*

[Sets the dish on a table.]

I am sure, sweet Kate, this kindness merits thanks.

*I am sure, sweet Kate, this kindness deserves
thanks.*

What! not a word? Nay, then thou lov'st it not,
And all my pains is sorted to no proof.
Here, take away this dish.

*What! Not a word? No, then you don't like it,
And all my trouble is for nothing.*

KATHERINA.
I pray you, let it stand.

Please, leave it there.

PETRUCHIO.
The poorest service is repaid with thanks;
And so shall mine, before you touch the meat.

The poorest service is repaid with thanks;
And so shall mine, before you touch the meat.

KATHERINA.
I thank you, sir.

I thank you, sir.

HORTENSIO.
Signior Petruchio, fie! you are to blame.
Come, Mistress Kate, I'll bear you company.

Sir Petuchio, enough! You are to blame.
Come, Madame Kate, I'll keep you company.

PETRUCHIO.
[Aside.]
Eat it up all, Hortensio, if thou lovest me.
Much good do it unto thy gentle heart!
Kate, eat apace: and now, my honey love,
Will we return unto thy father's house
And revel it as bravely as the best,
With silken coats and caps, and golden rings,
With ruffs and cuffs and farthingales and things;
With scarfs and fans and double change of bravery,

With amber bracelets, beads, and all this knavery.

What! hast thou din'd? The tailor stays thy leisure,

To deck thy body with his ruffling treasure.

Eat all of it up, Hortensio, if you are my friend.
May it do much good to your gentle heart!
Kate, eat after him: and now, my honey love,
We will return to your father's house
And enjoy it as well as the best,
With silk coats and hats, and golden rings,
With ruffs and cuffs and decorations and things;
With scarfs and fans and two changes of lovely
clothes,
With amber bracelets, beads, and a lot of other
stuff.
What, have you eaten? The tailor is here at your
convenience,
To decorate your body with his ruffled treasure.

[Enter TAILOR.]

Come, tailor, let us see these ornaments;
Lay forth the gown.--
Spread out the gown. --

[Enter HABERDASHER.]

[Enter HATMAKER.]

What news with you, sir?

What news with you, sir?

HABERDASHER.
Here is the cap your worship did bespeak.

Here is the cap your worship ordered.

PETRUCHIO.
Why, this was moulded on a porringer;
A velvet dish: fie, fie! 'tis lewd and filthy:

Why, 'tis a cockle or a walnut-shell,
A knack, a toy, a trick, a baby's cap:

Why, this looks like it was shaped on a bowl;
A velvet dish; enough, enough! It's improper and
dirty:
Why, it's a clam or a walnut shell,
A knickknack, a toy, a trick, a baby's cap:

Away with it! come, let me have a bigger.

Get rid of it! Come, let me have a bigger.

KATHERINA.
I'll have no bigger; this doth fit the time,
And gentlewomen wear such caps as these.

I don't want a bigger one; this one is fashionable,
And gentlewomen wear such caps as these.

PETRUCHIO.
When you are gentle, you shall have one too,
And not till then.

When you are gentle, you shall have one too,
And not till then.

HORTENSIO.
[Aside]
That will not be in haste.

That won't be any time soon.

KATHERINA.
Why, sir, I trust I may have leave to speak;
And speak I will. I am no child, no babe.
Your betters have endur'd me say my mind,

And if you cannot, best you stop your ears.

My tongue will tell the anger of my heart,
Or else my heart, concealing it, will break;
And rather than it shall, I will be free
Even to the uttermost, as I please, in words.

Why, sir, I trust I have permission to speak;
And I will speak. I am no child, no baby.
Men better than you have endured me speaking my
mind,
And if you cannot, then you should cover your
ears.
My tongue will tell the anger of my heart,
Or else my heart, hiding it, will break;
And rather than that happening, I will be free
No matter what, as I please, in words.

PETRUCHIO.
Why, thou say'st true; it is a paltry cap,
A custard-coffin, a bauble, a silken pie;
I love thee well in that thou lik'st it not.

Why, you are quite right; it is a pathetic cap,
A dessert dish, a little plaything, a silk pie;
I love you for not liking it.

KATHERINA.
Love me or love me not, I like the cap;
And it I will have, or I will have none.

Love me or do not love me, I like the cap;
And I want it, or I don't want any.

[Exit HABERDASHER.]

PETRUCHIO.
Thy gown? Why, ay: come, tailor, let us see't.
O mercy, God! what masquing stuff is here?
What's this? A sleeve? 'Tis like a demi-cannon.
What, up and down, carv'd like an appletart?
Here's snip and nip and cut and slish and slash,
Like to a censer in a barber's shop.
Why, what i' devil's name, tailor, call'st thou this?

Your gown? Why, yes: come, tailor, let us see it.
Oh mercy, God! What cheap costumery is here?
What's this? A sleeve? It's like a little cannon.
What, up and down, caved like an apple tart?
Here's snip and nip and cut and slish and slash,
As if it had been to a barber's shop.
Why, what in the davil's name, tailor, do you call
this?

HORTENSIO.
[Aside]
I see she's like to have neither cap nor gown.

I see she's likely to not get the cap or the gown.

TAILOR.
You bid me make it orderly and well,
According to the fashion and the time.

You told me to make it neatly and well,

PETRUCHIO.
Marry, and did; but if you be remember'd,
I did not bid you mar it to the time.
Go, hop me over every kennel home,
For you shall hop without my custom, sir.
I'll none of it: hence! make your best of it.

By Mary, I did; but if you remember,
I did not tell you to ruin it according to the time.
Go, jump over every doghouse home,
For I will not be your customer again, sir.
I'll have none of it: go! Make the best of it.

KATHERINA.
I never saw a better fashion'd gown,
More quaint, more pleasing, nor more commendable;
Belike you mean to make a puppet of me.

I never saw a better made gown,
More pretty, more pleasing, or more admirable;
It looks like you mean to make me into a puppet.

PETRUCHIO.
Why, true; he means to make a puppet of thee.

Why, it's true; he means to make a puppet out of
you.

TAILOR.
She says your worship means to make a puppet of her.

She says your worship means to make a puppet of
her.

PETRUCHIO.
O monstrous arrogance!
Thou liest, thou thread, thou thimble,
Thou yard, three-quarters, half-yard, quarter, nail!
Thou flea, thou nit, thou winter-cricket thou!
Brav'd in mine own house with a skein of thread!
Away! thou rag, thou quantity, thou remnant,
Or I shall so be-mete thee with thy yard
As thou shalt think on prating whilst thou liv'st!
I tell thee, I, that thou hast marr'd her gown.

O monstrous arrogance!
You lie, you thread, you thimble,
You yard, three-quarters, half-yard, quarter, nail!
You flea, you flea egg, you winter cricket you!
Standing in my own house with a skein of thread!
Away! You rag, you quantity, you remainder,
Or I will beat you with your yard
As you shall think of arguing while you live!
I tell you, I, that you have ruined her gown.

TAILOR.
Your worship is deceiv'd: the gown is made
Just as my master had direction.
Grumio gave order how it should be done.

Your worship is mistaken: the gown is made
Just as my master had directed.
Grumio gave order how it should be done.

GRUMIO.
I gave him no order; I gave him the stuff.

I gave him no order; I gave him the stuff.

TAILOR.
But how did you desire it should be made?

But how did you desire it should be made?

GRUMIO.
Marry, sir, with needle and thread.

Marry, sir, with needle and thread.

TAILOR.
But did you not request to have it cut?

But did you not request to have it cut?

GRUMIO.
Thou hast faced many things.

TAILOR.
I have.

GRUMIO.
Face not me. Thou hast braved many men; brave not me: I will neither be fac'd nor brav'd. I say unto thee, I bid thy master cut out the gown; but I did not bid him cut it to pieces: ergo, thou liest.

TAILOR.
Why, here is the note of the fashion to testify.

PETRUCHIO.
Read it.

GRUMIO.
The note lies in 's throat, if he say I said so.

TAILOR.
'Imprimis, a loose-bodied gown.'

GRUMIO.
Master, if ever I said loose-bodied gown, sew me in the skirts of it and beat me to death with a bottom

PETRUCHIO.
Proceed.

TAILOR.
'With a small compassed cape.'

GRUMIO.
I confess the cape.

TAILOR.
'With a trunk sleeve.'

GRUMIO.
I confess two sleeves.

TAILOR.
'The sleeves curiously cut.'

PETRUCHIO.
Ay, there's the villainy.

GRUMIO.

Thou hast faced many things.

I have.

Do not face me. You have braved many men; brave not me: I will neither be faced nor braved. I say to you, I told your master to cut out the gown; but I did not tell him to cut it to pieces: therefore, you are lying.

Why, here is a note of the directions to prove me right.

Read it.

The note lies in his throat, if he says I said so.

'First of all, a loose-bodied gown.'

Master, if I ever said 'loose-bodied gown', sew me into its skirts and beat me to death with a roll of brown thread; I said, 'a gown.'

Go ahead.

'With a small compassed cape.'

I admit to the cape.

'With a trunk sleeve.'

I admit to two sleeves.

'The sleeves uniquely cut.'

Yes, there's the problem.

Error i' the bill, sir; error i' the bill. I commanded the sleeves should be cut out, and sew'd up again; and that I'll prove upon thee, though thy little finger be armed in a thimble.

TAILOR.
This is true that I say;
an I had thee in place where thou shouldst know it.

GRUMIO.
I am for thee straight; take thou the bill, give me thy mete-yard, and spare not me.

HORTENSIO.
God-a-mercy, Grumio! Then he shall have no odds.

PETRUCHIO.
Well, sir, in brief, the gown is not for me

GRUMIO.
You are i' the right, sir; 'tis for my mistress.

PETRUCHIO.
Go, take it up unto thy master's use.

GRUMIO.
Villain, not for thy life!
Take up my mistress' gown for thy master's use!

PETRUCHIO.
Why, sir, what's your conceit in that?

GRUMIO.
O, sir, the conceit is deeper than you think for.
Take up my mistress' gown to his master's use!
O fie, fie, fie!

PETRUCHIO.
[Aside]
Hortensio, say thou wilt see the tailor paid.

[To Tailor.]
Go take it hence; be gone, and say no more.

HORTENSIO.
[Aside to Tailor.]
Tailor, I'll pay thee for thy gown to-morrow;
Take no unkindness of his hasty words.
Away, I say! commend me to thy master.

It's a mistake in the bill, sir; an error in the bill. I said the sleeves should be cut out, and sewed up again; and I'll prove that to you, even if your little finger is armed with a thimble.

I am telling the truth;
and I had you in a place where you should know it.

Fine, do you want to fight? Spare me nothing.

God-a-mercy, Grumio! Then he won't have a chance.

Well, sir, in brief, the gown is not for me

You are in the right, sir; it is for my lady.

Go, take it up for your master's use.

Villain, not for your life!
Take my lady's gown for your master's use!

Why, sir, what's your point in that?

Oh, sir, there is more meaning to it than you think.
Take up my lady's gown to his master's use!
Oh enough, enough, enough!

[Aside]
Hortensio, say you will make sure the tailor is paid.
[To Tailor.]
Go take it from here; be gone, and say no more.

Tailor, I'll pay your for your gown tomorrow;
Do not be offended personally by his hasty words.
Away, I say! Speak of you to your master.

[Exit TAILOR.]

PETRUCHIO.
Well, come, my Kate; we will unto your father's
Even in these honest mean habiliments.
Our purses shall be proud, our garments poor
For 'tis the mind that makes the body rich;
And as the sun breaks through the darkest clouds,
So honour peereth in the meanest habit.
What, is the jay more precious than the lark
Because his feathers are more beautiful?
Or is the adder better than the eel
Because his painted skin contents the eye?
O no, good Kate; neither art thou the worse
For this poor furniture and mean array.
If thou account'st it shame, lay it on me;
And therefore frolic; we will hence forthwith,
To feast and sport us at thy father's house.
Go call my men, and let us straight to him;
And bring our horses unto Long-lane end;
There will we mount, and thither walk on foot.

Let's see; I think 'tis now some seven o'clock,
And well we may come there by dinner-time.

KATHERINA.
I dare assure you, sir, 'tis almost two,
And 'twill be supper-time ere you come there.

PETRUCHIO.
It shall be seven ere I go to horse.
Look what I speak, or do, or think to do,

You are still crossing it. Sirs, let 't alone:
I will not go to-day; and ere I do,
It shall be what o'clock I say it is.

HORTENSIO.
Why, so this gallant will command the sun.

[Exeunt.]

Well, come, my Kate; we will go to your father's
Even in these honest, humble clothes.
Our purses shall be proud, our garments poor
For it is the mind that makes the body rich;
And as the sun breaks through the darkest clouds,
So honor peers through the most meager outfit.
What, is the jay more precious than the lark
Because his feathers are more beautiful?
Or is the adder better than the eel
Because his painted skin pleases the eye?
Oh no, good Kate, your are also none the worse
For this shabby appearance.
If you consider this shameful, blame it on me;
And therefore be happy; we will go soon,
To feast and have fun at your father's house.
Go call my men, and let us go straight to him;
And bring our horses to Long-land end;
There we will get on the horses, after walking
there
Let's see: I think it's now around seven o'clock,
And we will be in good time for dinner.

I can tell you, sir, it's almost two,
And it will be suppertime before you get there.

It will be seven before I go to the horse.
Pay attention to what I speak, or do, or think to
do,
Or are still going against it. Sirs, leave it alone:
I will not go today; and before I do,
It shall be what o'clock I say it is.

Why, this man wants to order around the sun.

Scene IV

Padua. Before BAPTISTA'S house

[Enter TRANIO, and the PEDANT dressed like VINCENTIO.]

TRANIO.
Sir, this is the house; please it you that I call?

Sir, this is the house; is it all right if I visit?

PEDANT.
Ay, what else? and, but I be deceived,
Signior Baptista may remember me,
Near twenty years ago in Genoa,
Where we were lodgers at the Pegasus.

Yes, what else? And, unless I am mistaken,
Signior Baptista may remember me,
From nearly twenty years ago in Genoa,
When we were guests staying at the Pegasus.

TRANIO.
'Tis well; and hold your own, in any case,
With such austerity as 'longeth to a father.

That's all right; and behave, in any case,
With such solemness as belongs to a father.

PEDANT.
I warrant you. But, sir, here comes your boy;
'Twere good he were school'd.

I promise to. But, sir, here comes your boy;
It would be best if he were informed.

[Enter BIONDELLO.]

TRANIO.
Fear you not him. Sirrah Biondello,
Now do your duty throughly, I advise you.
Imagine 'twere the right Vincentio.

Don't fear him. Biondello, young man,
Now do your duty throughly, I advise you.
Imagine this were the actual Vincentio.

BIONDELLO.
Tut! fear not me.

It's nothing! Don't worry about me.

TRANIO.
But hast thou done thy errand to Baptista?

But have you done your errand to Baptista?

BIONDELLO.
I told him that your father was at Venice,
And that you look'd for him this day in Padua.

I told him that your father was at Venice,
And that you were looking for him today in Padua.

TRANIO.
Thou'rt a tall fellow; hold thee that to drink.
Here comes Baptista. Set your countenance, sir.

You have done well; keep it up.
Here comes Baptista. Get ready, sir.

[Enter BAPTISTA and LUCENTIO.]

Signior Baptista, you are happily met.

Sir Baptista, you came at the perfect time.

[To the PEDANT]

Sir, this is the gentleman I told you of;
I pray you stand good father to me now;
Give me Bianca for my patrimony.

PEDANT.
Soft, son! Sir, by your leave: having come to Padua

To gather in some debts, my son Lucentio
Made me acquainted with a weighty cause
Of love between your daughter and himself:
And,--for the good report I hear of you,

And for the love he beareth to your daughter,
And she to him,--to stay him not too long,
I am content, in a good father's care,
To have him match'd; and, if you please to like

No worse than I, upon some agreement
Me shall you find ready and willing
With one consent to have her so bestow'd;
For curious I cannot be with you,
Signior Baptista, of whom I hear so well.

BAPTISTA.
Sir, pardon me in what I have to say.
Your plainness and your shortness please me well.
Right true it is your son Lucentio here
Doth love my daughter, and she loveth him,
Or both dissemble deeply their affections;
And therefore, if you say no more than this,
And pass my daughter a sufficient dower,

The match is made, and all is done:
Your son shall have my daughter with consent.

TRANIO.
I thank you, sir.
Where then do you know best
We be affied, and such assurance ta'en
As shall with either part's agreement stand?

BAPTISTA.
Not in my house, Lucentio, for you know
Pitchers have ears, and I have many servants;
Besides, old Gremio is hearkening still,
And happily we might be interrupted.

TRANIO.

Sir, this is the gentleman I told you of;
Please be a good father to me now;
Let me have Bianca.

Hush, son! Sir, begging your pardon: having come to Padua
To gather in some debts, my son Lucentio
Let me know about the serious issue
Of love between your daughter and himself:
And, -- because of the good reputation I hear of you,
And for the love he holds for your daughter,
And she to him, -- to not make him wait too long,
I am content, like a good father,
To have him married; and, if you are pleased to like
No worse than I, upon some agreement
Me shall you find ready and willing
With permission to have her granted in marriage;
For I cannot be suspicious of you,
Signior Baptista, of whom I hear so well.

Sir, pardon me in what I have to say.
Your plain talk and short speech please me well.
It is true that your son Lucentio here
Loves my daughter, and she loves him,
Or they are both faking their emotions very well;
That like a father you will deal with him,
And pass onto my daughter a large enough inheritance,
The match is made, and all is done:
Your son shall have my daughter with consent.

I thank you, sir.
Where then do you know best
Where we can set down the legal contract
That we agree upon each party's actions?

Not in my house, Lucentio, for you know
Pitchers have ears, and I have many servants;
Besides, old Gremio is still longing for her,
And we might unluckily be interrupted.

Then at my lodging, an it like you:
There doth my father lie; and there this night
We'll pass the business privately and well.
Send for your daughter by your servant here;
My boy shall fetch the scrivener presently.
The worst is this, that at so slender warning

You are like to have a thin and slender pittance.

BAPTISTA.
It likes me well. Cambio, hie you home,
And bid Bianca make her ready straight;
And, if you will, tell what hath happened:
Lucentio's father is arriv'd in Padua,
And how she's like to be Lucentio's wife.

LUCENTIO.
I pray the gods she may, with all my heart!

TRANIO.
Dally not with the gods, but get thee gone.
Signior Baptista, shall I lead the way? Welcome!
One mess is like to be your cheer; come, sir;
we will better it in Pisa.

BAPTISTA.
I follow you.

[Exeunt TRANIO, Pedant, and BAPTISTA.]

BIONDELLO.
Cambio!

LUCENTIO.
What say'st thou, Biondello?

BIONDELLO.
You saw my master wink and laugh upon you?

LUCENTIO.
Biondello, what of that?

BIONDELLO.
Faith, nothing; but has left me here behind to
expound the meaning or moral of his signs and
tokens.

LUCENTIO.
I pray thee moralize them.

Then at my place, if that is all right:
My father is staying; and there, tonight
We'll settle this business privately and well.
Send for your daughter by your servant here;
My boy shall fetch the official in a moment.
The worst thing about this, that at such short
notice
You are likely to not get a big fee.

I like this plan. Cambio, get home,
And tell Bianca to get herself ready;
And, if you will, tell her what has happened:
Lucentio's father has arrived in Padua,
And how she's going to be Lucentio's wife.

I pray the gods she may, with all my heart!

Do not mess with the gods, but get yourself gone.
Sir Baptista, shall I lead the way? Welcome!
It may not be up to your standards, but come, sir;
we will make it better in Pisa.

I follow you.

Cambio!

What do you have to say, Biondello?

You saw my master wink and laugh at you?

Biondello, what about it?

Faith, nothing; but it has left me here to ponder
the meaning or moral of his signs and gestures.

Please explain them.

BIONDELLO.
Then thus: Baptista is safe, talking with the deceiving
father of a deceitful son.

LUCENTIO.
And what of him?

BIONDELLO.
His daughter is to be brought by you to the supper.

LUCENTIO.
And then?

BIONDELLO.
The old priest at Saint Luke's church is at your
command at all hours.

LUCENTIO.
And what of all this?

BIONDELLO.
I cannot tell, except they are busied about a
counterfeit assurance. Take your assurance of her,
cum privilegio ad imprimendum solum; to the
church! take the priest, clerk, and some sufficient
honest witnesses.

[Going.]

LUCENTIO.
Hear'st thou, Biondello?

BIONDELLO.
I cannot tarry: I knew a wench married in an
afternoon as she went to the garden for parsley to
stuff a rabbit; and so may you, sir; and so adieu, sir.
My master hath appointed me to go to Saint Luke's
to bid the priest be ready to come against you,
come with your appendix.

[Exit.]

LUCENTIO.
I may, and will, if she be so contented.
She will be pleas'd; then wherefore should I doubt?
Hap what hap may, I'll roundly go about her;
It shall go hard if Cambio go without her.

[Exit.]

---

*Then this is how it is: Baptista is safe,
talking with the fake father of a fake son.*

And what of him?

His daughter is to be brought by you to the supper.

And then?

*The old priest at Saint Luke's church is at your
command at all hours.*

And what of all this?

*I cannot tell, except they are busy putting together
a false promise. Take your promise of her,
to the church! Take the priest, clerk, and enough
honest witnesses. If this is not what you look for,
I have more to say, But say goodbye to Bianca
forever and a day.*

Do you hear, Biondello?

*I cannot stay: I knew a girl married in an
afternoon as she went to the garden for pars
to stuff a rabbit; and so may you, sir; and so
goodbye, sir. My master has told me to go to
Saint Luke's to tell the priest to be ready to come
against you, come with your book.*

*I may, and will, if that's what she wants.
She will be pleased; then why should I doubt?
Come what me, I'll go around her;
It will turn out badly if Cambio goes without her.*

Scene V

A public road

[Enter PETRUCHIO, KATHERINA, HORTENSIO, and SERVANTS.]

PETRUCHIO.
Come on, i' God's name; once more toward our
father's. Good Lord, how bright and goodly
shines the moon!

Come on, in God's name; once more toward our
father's. Good Lord, the moon shines so bright
and well!

KATHERINA.
The moon! The sun; it is not moonlight now.

The moon! The sun; it is not moonlight now.

PETRUCHIO.
I say it is the moon that shines so bright.

I say it is the moon that shines so bright.

KATHERINA.
I know it is the sun that shines so bright.

I know it is the sun that shines so bright.

PETRUCHIO.
Now by my mother's son, and that's myself,
It shall be moon, or star, or what I list,
Or ere I journey to your father's house.
Go on and fetch our horses back again.
Evermore cross'd and cross'd; nothing but cross'd!

Now by my mother's son, and that's myself,
It shall be moon, or star, or what I say,
Or before I journey to your father's house.
Go on and fetch our horses back again.
Always fought against and against; nothing but
against!

HORTENSIO.
Say as he says, or we shall never go.

Say as he says, or we shall never go.

KATHERINA.
Forward, I pray, since we have come so far,

And be it moon, or sun, or what you please;

And if you please to call it a rush-candle,
Henceforth I vow it shall be so for me.

Let us go forward, please, since we have come so
far,
And let it be moon, or sun, or whatever you
please;
And if you wish to call it a candle,
From now on I swear that's what it will be for me.

PETRUCHIO.
I say it is the moon.

I say it is the moon.

KATHERINA.
I know it is the moon.

I know it is the moon.

PETRUCHIO.
Nay, then you lie; it is the blessed sun.

No, you are lying; it is the blessed sun.

KATHERINA.

Then, God be bless'd, it is the blessed sun;
But sun it is not when you say it is not,
And the moon changes even as your mind.
What you will have it nam'd, even that it is,
And so it shall be so for Katherine.

HORTENSIO.
Petruchio, go thy ways; the field is won.

PETRUCHIO.
Well, forward, forward! thus the bowl should run,

And not unluckily against the bias.
But, soft! Company is coming here.

[Enter VINCENTIO, in a travelling dress.]

[To VINCENTIO]

Good-morrow, gentle mistress; where away?
Tell me, sweet Kate, and tell me truly too,
Hast thou beheld a fresher gentlewoman?
Such war of white and red within her cheeks!

What stars do spangle heaven with such beauty
As those two eyes become that heavenly face?
Fair lovely maid, once more good day to thee.

Sweet Kate, embrace her for her beauty's sake.

HORTENSIO.
'A will make the man mad, to make a woman of him.

KATHERINA.
Young budding virgin, fair and fresh and sweet,

Whither away, or where is thy abode?
Happy the parents of so fair a child;

Happier the man whom favourable stars

Allot thee for his lovely bed-fellow.

PETRUCHIO.
Why, how now, Kate! I hope thou art not mad:

This is a man, old, wrinkled, faded, wither'd,
And not a maiden, as thou sayst he is.

KATHERINA.

Then, God be blessed, it is the blessed sun;
But it is not the sun when you say it is not,
And the moon changes the way your mind does.
What you will call it, that is what it is,
And that is how it shall be for Katherine.

Petruchio, move on; the battle is won.

Well forward, forward! This is how things should work,
And not always against the grain.
But, hush! Someone is coming here.

Good day, gentle miss; where your going?
Tell me, sweet Kate, and tell me truly too,
Have you ever seen a prettier young woman?
Such a war between white and red coloring in her cheeks!
What stars decorate the sky with such beauty
As those two eyes suit that heavenly face?
Beautiful lovely maiden, once more a good day to you.
Sweet Kate, give her a hug for being so beautiful.

You will drive the man crazy, calling him a woman.

Young blooming maiden, pretty and fresh and sweet,
Where are you going, or where is your home?
The parents of such a beautiful child must be happy;
And even happier must be the man whose good luck
Makes you his lovely wife.

Why, what's going on, Kate! I hope you are not insane:
This is a man, old, wrinkled, faded, withered,
And not a maiden, as you say he is.

Pardon, old father, my mistaking eyes,
That have been so bedazzled with the sun
That everything I look on seemeth green:
Now I perceive thou art a reverend father;
Pardon, I pray thee, for my mad mistaking.

PETRUCHIO.
Do, good old grandsire, and withal make known
Which way thou travellest: if along with us,

We shall be joyful of thy company.

VINCENTIO.
Fair sir, and you my merry mistress,
That with your strange encounter much amaz'd me,

My name is called Vincentio; my dwelling Pisa;
And bound I am to Padua, there to visit
A son of mine, which long I have not seen.

PETRUCHIO.
What is his name?

VINCENTIO.
Lucentio, gentle sir.

PETRUCHIO.
Happily met; the happier for thy son.

And now by law, as well as reverend age,
I may entitle thee my loving father:
The sister to my wife, this gentlewoman,
Thy son by this hath married. Wonder not,

Nor be not griev'd: she is of good esteem,
Her dowry wealthy, and of worthy birth;
Beside, so qualified as may beseem

The spouse of any noble gentleman.
Let me embrace with old Vincentio;
And wander we to see thy honest son,
Who will of thy arrival be full joyous.

VINCENTIO.
But is this true? or is it else your pleasure,
Like pleasant travellers, to break a jest
Upon the company you overtake?

HORTENSIO.
I do assure thee, father, so it is.

Pardon, old father, my mistaking eyes,
That have been so blinded by the sun
That everything I look at seems young:
Now I can see you are a dignified father;
Forgive me, please, for my crazy mistake.

Do, good old grandfather, and also tell us
Which way you are traveling: if it is the same as us,
We shall be glad of the company.

Good sir, and you my playful lady,
That with your strange behavior has amazed me very much,
My name is Vincenio; my home is Pisa;
And I am going to Padua, to visit there
A son of mine, who I have not seen for a long time.

What is his name?

Lucentio, gentle sir.

How fortunate a coincidence; even luckier for your son.
And now by law, as well as your respectable age,
I may call you my loving father:
The sister of my wife, this noblewoman,
Has married your son by this time. Do not be surprised,
And do not be sad: she has a good reputation,
Her dowry is great, and she is from fine family;
Besides that, she has at the qualities that are approrpriate
For the wife of any noble gentleman.
Let me embrace with old Vincentio;
And let us go travel to see your honest son,
Who will be joyful to see you.

But is this true, or else is it your habit;
Like teasing travelers, to make a joke
With the company you come across?

I do assure you, father, this is true.

PETRUCHIO.
Come, go along, and see the truth hereof;
For our first merriment hath made thee jealous.

[Exeunt all but HORTENSIO.]

HORTENSIO.
Well, Petruchio, this has put me in heart.
Have to my widow! and if she be froward,
Then hast thou taught Hortensio to be untoward.

[Exit.]

Come, go along, and see the truth of it;
For our first joke has made you suspicious.

Well, Petruchio, this has encouraged me.
Now I will go to my widow! And if she is difficult,
You have taught Hortensio how to be stubborn.

ACT V

Scene I

Padua. Before LUCENTIO'S house

[Enter on one side BIONDELLO, LUCENTIO, and BIANCA; GREMIO walking on other side.]

BIONDELLO.
Softly and swiftly, sir, for the priest is ready.

Quietly and quickly, sir, for the priest is ready.

LUCENTIO.
I fly, Biondello; but they may chance to need
thee at home, therefore leave us.

*I will hurry, Biondello; but it is possible they will
need you at home, therefore leave us.*

BIONDELLO.
Nay, faith, I'll see the church o' your back;
and then come back to my master's as soon as I can.

*No, by my faith, I will see you to the church;
and then come back to my master's as soon as I
can.*

[Exeunt LUCENTIO, BIANCA, and BIONDELLO.]

GREMIO.
I marvel Cambio comes not all this while.

*I am amazed Cambio has not shown up in all this
time.*

[Enter PETRUCHIO, KATHERINA, VINCENTIO, and ATTENDANTS.]

PETRUCHIO.
Sir, here's the door; this is Lucentio's house:
My father's bears more toward the market-place;
Thither must I, and here I leave you, sir.

*Sir, here's the door; this is Lucentio's house:
My father's is closer to the market-place;
I must go there, and here I leave you, sir.*

VINCENTIO.
You shall not choose but drink before you go.
I think I shall command your welcome here,
And by all likelihood some cheer is toward.

*You should have a drink before you go.
I think I shall demand that you be invited here,
And it is likely you will be most welcome.*

[Knocks.]

GREMIO.
They're busy within; you were best knock louder.

They're busy inside; you should knock louder.

[Enter PEDANT above, at a window.]

PEDANT.
What's he that knocks as he would beat down the gate?

*Who is he that knocks as if he would beat down the
gate?*

VINCENTIO.
Is Signior Lucentio within, sir?

Is Sir Lucentio inside, sir?

PEDANT.

He's within, sir, but not to be spoken withal.

VINCENTIO.
What if a man bring him a hundred pound or two to
make merry withal?

PEDANT.
Keep your hundred pounds to yourself:
he shall need none so long as I live.

PETRUCHIO.
Nay, I told you your son was well beloved in Padua.
Do you hear, sir? To leave frivolous circumstances,
I pray you tell Signior Lucentio that his father is come
from Pisa, and is here at the door to speak with him.

PEDANT.
Thou liest: his father is come from Padua,
and here looking out at the window.

VINCENTIO.
Art thou his father?

PEDANT.
Ay, sir; so his mother says, if I may believe her.

PETRUCHIO.
[To VINCENTIO]
Why, how now, gentleman! why, this is flat knavery
to take upon you another man's name.

PEDANT.
Lay hands on the villain: I believe 'a means to cozen
somebody in this city under my countenance.

[Re-enter BIONDELLO.]

BIONDELLO.
I have seen them in the church together: God send 'em
good shipping! But who is here? Mine old master,
Vincentio! Now we are undone and brought to nothing.

VINCENTIO.
[Seeing BIONDELLO.]
Come hither, crack-hemp.

BIONDELLO.
I hope I may choose, sir.

VINCENTIO.

*He's inside, sir, but is not available to be spoken
to right now.*

*What if a man brings him a hundred pounds or
two to enjoy himself with?*

*Keep your hundred pounds to yourself:
he shall need none so long as I live.*

*No, I told you your son was well-liked in Padua.
Do you hear, sir? To cut to the chase, please tell
Sir Lucentio that his father has come from Pisa,
and is here at the door to speak with him.*

*You're lying: his father has come from Padua,
and is here looking out the window.*

Are you his father?

Yes, sir; his mother says so, if I may believe her.

*Why, what's going on, man?! Why, this is trickery
to take upon yourself another man's name.*

*Catch the villain: I believe he means to cheat
somebody in this city under my countenance.*

*I have seen them in the church together: God give
them luck! But who is here? My old master,
Vincentio! Now we are ruined and all our plans
are for nothing.*

Come here, cracked-head.

I hope I may choose, sir.

Come hither, you rogue. What, have you forgot me?

BIONDELLO.
Forgot you! No, sir: I could not forget you,
for I never saw you before in all my life.

VINCENTIO.
What, you notorious villain! didst thou never see
thy master's father, Vincentio?

BIONDELLO.
What, my old worshipful old master? Yes, marry, sir;
see where he looks out of the window.

VINCENTIO.
Is't so, indeed?

[He beats BIONDELLO.]

BIONDELLO.
Help, help, help! here's a madman will murder me.

[Exit.]

PEDANT.
Help, son! help, Signior Baptista!

[Exit from the window.]

PETRUCHIO.
Prithee, Kate, let's stand aside and see the end of
this controversy.

[They retire.]

[Re-enter PEDANT below; BAPTISTA, TRANIO, and SERVANTS.]

TRANIO.
Sir, what are you that offer to beat my servant?

VINCENTIO.
What am I, sir! nay, what are you, sir? O immortal
gods! O fine villain! A silken doublet, a velvet hose,
a scarlet cloak, and a copatain hat! O, I am undone!
I am undone! While I play the good husband at home,
my son and my servant spend all at the university.

TRANIO.
How now! what's the matter?

---

*Come hither, you rogue. What, have you forgot
me?*

*Forgot you! No, sir: I could not forget you,
for I never saw you before in all my life.*

*What, you terrible villain! Did you never see
your master's father, Vincentio?*

*What, my old respectable old master? Yes, by
Mary, sir; she where he looks out of the window.*

Is that so, indeed?

*Help, help, help! Here's a madman that will
murder me.*

Help, son! help, Signior Baptista!

*Please, Kate, let's stand to the side and see the
end of this conflict.*

Sir, who are you that tries to beat my servant?

*What am I, sir? No, what are you, sir? Oh
immortal gods! Oh great villain! A silk doublet,
velvet stockings, a scarlet clock, and a fancy hat!
Oh, I am ruined! I am ruined! While I play the
good husband at home, my son and my servant
spend all their money at the university.*

What's going on? What's the matter?

BAPTISTA.
What, is the man lunatic?

What, is the man insane?

TRANIO.
Sir, you seem a sober ancient gentleman by your habit,
but your words show you a madman. Why, sir, what
'cerns it you if I wear pearl and gold? I thank my good
father, I am able to maintain it.

*Sir, you seem a serious elderly gentleman by your
clothes, but your words show you to be a madman.
Why, sir, what business is it of yours if I wear
pearls and gold? I thank my good father that I can
afford it.*

VINCENTIO.
Thy father! O villain! he is a sailmaker in Bergamo.

*Your father! Oh villain! He is a sailmaker in
Bergamo.*

BAPTISTA.
You mistake, sir; you mistake, sir. Pray,
what do you think is his name?

*You are mistaken, sir; you are mistaken, sir.
Please, what do you think is his name?*

VINCENTIO.
His name! As if I knew not his name!
I have brought him up ever since he was three years
old, and his name is Tranio.

*His name! As if I did not know his name!
I have brought him up ever since he was three
years old, and his name is Tranio.*

PEDANT.
Away, away, mad ass! His name is Lucentio;
and he is mine only son, and heir to the lands of me,
Signior Vicentio.

*Away, away, mad fool! His name is Lucentio;
and he is my only son, and the heir to the lands of
me, Sir Vicentio.*

VINCENTIO.
Lucentio! O, he hath murdered his master!
Lay hold on him, I charge you, in the Duke's name.
O, my son, my son! Tell me, thou villain,
where is my son, Lucentio?

*Lucentio! Oh, he has murdered his master!
Capture him, I order you, in the Duke's name.
Oh, my son, my son! Tell me, you villain,
where is my son, Lucentio?*

TRANIO.
Call forth an officer.

Call forth an officer.

[Enter one with an OFFICER.]

Carry this mad knave to the gaol. Father Baptista,
I charge you see that he be forthcoming.

*Carry this insane man to the jail. Father Baptista,
I ask you to make sure it happens.*

VINCENTIO.
Carry me to the gaol!

Carry me to the jail?!

GREMIO.
Stay, officer; he shall not go to prison.

Stay, officer; he shall not go to prison.

BAPTISTA.
Talk not, Signior Gremio; I say he shall go to prison.

Be quiet, Sir Gremio; I say he shall go to prison.

GREMIO.

Take heed, Signior Baptista, lest you be cony-catched
in this business; I dare swear this is the right Vincentio.

*Listen, Sir Baptista, so you don't get tricked in this
business; I think this really is the correct
Vincentio.*

PEDANT.
Swear if thou darest.

Swear if you dare.

GREMIO.
Nay, I dare not swear it.

No, I don't dare swear it.

TRANIO.
Then thou wert best say that I am not Lucentio.

*Then it would be best for you to say that I am not
Lucentio.*

GREMIO.
Yes, I know thee to be Signior Lucentio.

Yes, I know you to be Sir Lucentio.

BAPTISTA.
Away with the dotard! to the gaol with him!

*Away with the senile old man! To the jail with
him!*

VINCENTIO.
Thus strangers may be haled and abus'd:
O monstrous villain!

*This is how strangers may be greeted and abused:
oh monstrous villain!*

[Re-enter BIONDELLO, with LUCENTIO and BIANCA.]

BIONDELLO.
O! we are spoiled; and yonder he is:
deny him, forswear him, or else we are all undone.

*Oh! We are spoiled; and he is over there:
get rid of him, or else we are all ruined.*

LUCENTIO.
[Kneeling.]
Pardon, sweet father.

Pardon, sweet father.

VINCENTIO.
Lives my sweetest son?

Is my sweetest son alive?

[BIONDELLO, TRANIO, and PEDANT, run out.]

BIANCA.
[Kneeling.]
Pardon, dear father.

Pardon, dear father.

BAPTISTA.
How hast thou offended? Where is Lucentio?

What have you done wrong? Where is Lucentio?

LUCENTIO.
Here's Lucentio,
Right son to the right Vincentio;
That have by marriage made thy daughter mine,

While counterfeit supposes blear'd thine eyne.

*Here's Lucentio,
The actual son of the actual Vincentio;
That has married your daughter and made your
daughter mine,
While lies and tricks confused you.*

GREMIO.
Here 's packing, with a witness, to deceive us all!

Here's the truth, with a witness, to fool us all!

VINCENTIO.
Where is that damned villain, Tranio,
That fac'd and brav'd me in this matter so?

Where is that damned villain, Tranio,
That faced and braved me in this business so
much?

BAPTISTA.
Why, tell me, is not this my Cambio?

Why, tell me, is not this my Cambio?

BIANCA.
Cambio is chang'd into Lucentio.

Cambio has changed to Lucentio.

LUCENTIO.
Love wrought these miracles. Bianca's love
Made me exchange my state with Tranio,
While he did bear my countenance in the town;

And happily I have arriv'd at the last
Unto the wished haven of my bliss.
What Tranio did, myself enforc'd him to;
Then pardon him, sweet father, for my sake.

Love made these miracles. Bianca's love
Made me exchange my position in life with Tranio,
While he held up my duties and identity in the
town;
And fortunately I have arrived at last
To the wished safe home of my bliss.
What Tranio did, I ordered him to;
Then pardon him, sweet father, for my sake.

VINCENTIO.
I'll slit the villain's nose that would have sent me to
the gaol.

I'll slit the villain's nose that would have sent me
to the gaol.

BAPTISTA.
[To LUCENTIO.]
But do you hear, sir? Have you married my daughter
without asking my good will?

But do you hear, sir? Have you married my
daughter without asking my good will?

VINCENTIO.
Fear not, Baptista; we will content you, go to:
but I will in, to be revenged for this villainy.

Don't worry, Baptista; we will make it right for
you: but I will be involved, to get revenge for this
villainy.

[Exit.]

BAPTISTA.
And I to sound the depth of this knavery.

And I to see the full extent of this trickery.

[Exit.]

LUCENTIO.
Look not pale, Bianca; thy father will not frown.

Don't look pale, Bianca; your father will come
around.

[Exeunt LUCENTIO and BIANCA.]

GREMIO.

My cake is dough, but I'll in among the rest;
Out of hope of all but my share of the feast.

I will gain nothing, but I'll join in among the rest;
Not hoping for anything but my share of the feast.

[Exit.]

[PETRUCHIO and KATHERINA advance.]

KATHERINA.
Husband, let's follow to see the end of this ado.

Husband, let's follow to see the end of this
business.

PETRUCHIO.
First kiss me, Kate, and we will.

First kiss me, Kate, and we will.

KATHERINA.
What! in the midst of the street?

What! in the midst of the street?

PETRUCHIO.
What! art thou ashamed of me?

What! Are you ashamed of me?

KATHERINA.
No, sir; God forbid; but ashamed to kiss.

No, sir; God forbid; but ashamed to kiss.

PETRUCHIO.
Why, then, let's home again. Come, sirrah, let's away.

Why, then, let's go go home again. Come, man,
let's head out.

KATHERINA.
Nay, I will give thee a kiss: now pray thee, love, stay.

No, I will give you a kiss: now please, love, stay.

PETRUCHIO.
Is not this well? Come, my sweet Kate:
Better once than never, for never too late.

Isn't this wonderful? Come, my sweet Kate:
Better once than never, for never too late.

[Exeunt.]

Scene II

A room in LUCENTIO'S house

[Enter BAPTISTA, VINCENTIO, GREMIO, the PEDANT, LUCENTIO, BIANCA, PETRUCHIO, KATHERINA, HORTENSIO, and WIDOW. TRANIO, BIONDELLO, and GRUMIO, and Others, attending.]

LUCENTIO.
At last, though long, our jarring notes agree:

And time it is when raging war is done,
To smile at 'scapes and perils overblown.

My fair Bianca, bid my father welcome,
While I with self-same kindness welcome thine.

Brother Petruchio, sister Katherina,
And thou, Hortensio, with thy loving widow,
Feast with the best, and welcome to my house:
My banquet is to close our stomachs up,
After our great good cheer. Pray you, sit down;

For now we sit to chat as well as eat.

[They sit at table.]

PETRUCHIO.
Nothing but sit and sit, and eat and eat!

BAPTISTA.
Padua affords this kindness, son Petruchio.

PETRUCHIO.
Padua affords nothing but what is kind.

HORTENSIO.
For both our sakes I would that word were true.

PETRUCHIO.
Now, for my life, Hortensio fears his widow.

WIDOW.
Then never trust me if I be afeard.

PETRUCHIO.
You are very sensible, and yet you miss my sense:

At last, though it took a long time, we have settled our disagreements:
And it is time, once raging war has ended,
To smile at escapades and dangers we have survived.
My beautiful Bianca, welcome my father,
While I with the very same kindness welcome yours.
Brother Petruchio, sister Katherina,
And you, Hortensio, with your loving widow,
Feast with the best, and welcome to my house:
My banquet is to fill up our stomachs,
After our great happiness and celebration. Please, sit down;
For now we sit to chat as well as eat.

Nothing but sit and sit, and eat and eat!

Padua gives us this kindness, son Petruchio.

Padua gives nothing but what is kind.

For both our sakes I would that word were true.

Now, for my life, Hortensio fears his widow.

Then never thrust me if I am afraid.

You are very sensible, and yet you miss my sense:

I mean Hortensio is afeard of you.

WIDOW.
He that is giddy thinks the world turns round.

PETRUCHIO.
Roundly replied.

KATHERINA.
Mistress, how mean you that?

WIDOW.
Thus I conceive by him.

PETRUCHIO.
Conceives by me! How likes Hortensio that?

HORTENSIO.
My widow says thus she conceives her tale.

PETRUCHIO.
Very well mended. Kiss him for that, good widow.

KATHERINA.
'He that is giddy thinks the world turns round':
I pray you tell me what you meant by that.

WIDOW.
Your husband, being troubled with a shrew,
Measures my husband's sorrow by his woe;
And now you know my meaning.

KATHERINA.
A very mean meaning.

WIDOW.
Right, I mean you.

KATHERINA.
And I am mean, indeed, respecting you.

PETRUCHIO.
To her, Kate!

HORTENSIO.
To her, widow!

PETRUCHIO.
A hundred marks, my Kate does put her down.

I mean Hortensio is afraid of you.

He that is dizzy thinks the world is spinning around.

Good answer.

Madame, what do you mean?

That's how I conceive by him.

Conceives by me! How does Hortensio like that?

My widow says this is how she conceives her story.

That's a good fix. Kiss him for that, good widow.

*'He that is giddy thinks the world turns round':
Please tell me what you meant by that.*

*Your husband, being troubled with a shrew,
Compares my husband's troubles by his suffering;
And now you know my meaning.*

A very mean meaning.

Right, I mean you.

And I am mean, indeed, respecting you.

To her, Kate!

To her, widow!

A hundred marks, my Kate does put her down.

HORTENSIO.
That's my office.

That's my job.

PETRUCHIO.
Spoke like an officer: ha' to thee, lad.

Spoken like an officer: here's to you, young man.

[Drinks to HORTENSIO.]

BAPTISTA.
How likes Gremio these quick-witted folks?

How does Gremio like these quick-witted folks?

GREMIO.
Believe me, sir, they butt together well.

Believe me, sir, they butt together well.

BIANCA.
Head and butt! An hasty-witted body
Would say your head and butt were head and horn.

Head and butt! Someone in a rush
Would say your head and butt were head and
horn.

VINCENTIO.
Ay, mistress bride, hath that awaken'd you?

Ah, madam bride, has that awakened you?

BIANCA.
Ay, but not frighted me; therefore I'll sleep again.

Yes, but not frightened me; therefore I'll sleep
again.

PETRUCHIO.
Nay, that you shall not; since you have begun,
Have at you for a bitter jest or two.

No, you shall not do that; since you have begun,
You need to make a few sharp jokes.

BIANCA.
Am I your bird?
I mean to shift my bush,
And then pursue me as you draw your bow.
You are welcome all.

Am I your bird?
I mean to move my nest,
And then you can chase me as you draw your bow.
You are welcome all.

[Exeunt BIANCA, KATHERINA, and WIDOW.]

PETRUCHIO.
She hath prevented me.
Here, Signior Tranio;
This bird you aim'd at, though you hit her not:
Therefore a health to all that shot and miss'd.

She has prevented me.
Here, Sir Tranio;
You aimed at this bird, though you did not hit her:
Therefore I drink to all that shot and missed.

TRANIO.
O, sir! Lucentio slipp'd me like his greyhound,
Which runs himself, and catches for his master.

Oh, sir! Lucentio sent me like I was his greyhound,
Who runs himself, and catches for his master.

PETRUCHIO.
A good swift simile, but something currish.

A good analogy, but sounds a bit doggish.

TRANIO.

'Tis well, sir, that you hunted for yourself:
'Tis thought your deer does hold you at a bay.

BAPTISTA.
O ho, Petruchio! Tranio hits you now.

LUCENTIO.
I thank thee for that gird, good Tranio.

HORTENSIO.
Confess, confess; hath he not hit you here?

PETRUCHIO.
A' has a little gall'd me, I confess;
And, as the jest did glance away from me,
'Tis ten to one it maim'd you two outright.

BAPTISTA.
Now, in good sadness, son Petruchio,
I think thou hast the veriest shrew of all.

PETRUCHIO.
Well, I say no; and therefore, for assurance,
Let's each one send unto his wife,
And he whose wife is most obedient,
To come at first when he doth send for her,
Shall win the wager which we will propose.

HORTENSIO.
Content. What's the wager?

LUCENTIO.
Twenty crowns.

PETRUCHIO.
Twenty crowns!
I'll venture so much of my hawk or hound,
But twenty times so much upon my wife.

LUCENTIO.
A hundred then.

HORTENSIO.
Content.

PETRUCHIO.
A match! 'tis done.

HORTENSIO.
Who shall begin?

It's good, sir, that you hunted for yourself:
Though it is thought that now your deer has you trapped.

Oh, ha, Petruchio! Tranio hits you now.

I thank you for that jab, good Tranio.

Confess, confess; has he not hit you here?

He has annoyed me a little, I confess;
And, as the joke just bounced away from me,
It is ten to one it stabbed you straight on.

Now, in all seriousness, son Petruchio,
I think you have the worst shrew of all.

Well, I say no; and therefore, for confirmation,
Let each one call for his wife,
And he whose wife is most obedient,
To come first when he sends for her,
Shall win the bet which we will make.

Sounds good. What's the bet?

Twenty crowns.

Twenty crowns!
I'd bet as much on one of my hawks or hounds,
But twenty times that much on my wife.

A hundred then.

Sounds good.

We have agreed, then!

Who shall begin?

LUCENTIO.
That will I.
Go, Biondello, bid your mistress come to me.

I will.
Go, Biondello, tell your lady to come to me.

BIONDELLO.
I go.

I go.

[Exit.]

BAPTISTA.
Son, I'll be your half, Bianca comes.

Son, I'll be your half, Bianca comes.

LUCENTIO.
I'll have no halves; I'll bear it all myself.

I'll have no halves; I'll hold it all myself.

[Re-enter BIONDELLO.]

How now! what news?

What's going on? What news?

BIONDELLO.
Sir, my mistress sends you word
That she is busy and she cannot come.

Sir, my lady replies
That she is busy and she cannot come.

PETRUCHIO.
How! She's busy, and she cannot come!
Is that an answer?

Huh! She's busy, and she cannot come!
Is that an answer?

GREMIO.
Ay, and a kind one too:
pray God, sir, your wife send you not a worse.

Yes, and a kind one too:
pray God, sir, your wife does not send you a worse
one.

PETRUCHIO.
I hope, better.

I hope, better.

HORTENSIO.
Sirrah Biondello, go and entreat my wife
To come to me forthwith.

Sir Biondello, go and plead with my wife
To come to me right now.

[Exit BIONDELLO.]

PETRUCHIO.
O, ho! entreat her! Nay, then she must needs come.

Oh, ha! Plead with her! No, then she must come.

HORTENSIO.
I am afraid, sir,
Do what you can, yours will not be entreated.

I am afraid, sir,
Do what you can, yours will not be entreated.

[Re-enter BIONDELLO.]

Now, where's my wife?

Now, where's my wife?

BIONDELLO.
She says you have some goodly jest in hand:
She will not come; she bids you come to her.

She says she knows it is some kind of joke:
She will not come; she tells you to come to her.

PETRUCHIO.
Worse and worse; she will not come! O vile,
Intolerable, not to be endur'd!
Sirrah Grumio, go to your mistress; say,
I command her come to me.

Worse and worse; she will not come! O terrible,
Intolerable, not to be endured!
Grumio, my man, go to your lady; say,
I command her come to me.

[Exit GRUMIO.]

HORTENSIO.
I know her answer.

I know her answer.

PETRUCHIO.
What?

What?

HORTENSIO.
She will not.

She will not.

PETRUCHIO.
The fouler fortune mine, and there an end.

That will be bad luck for me, and that would be
the end.

[Re-enter KATHERINA.]

BAPTISTA.
Now, by my holidame, here comes Katherina!

Now, by my holy mother, here comes Katherina!

KATHERINA.
What is your sir, that you send for me?

What is your sir, that you send for me?

PETRUCHIO.
Where is your sister, and Hortensio's wife?

Where is your sister, and Hortensio's wife?

KATHERINA.
They sit conferring by the parlour fire.

They sit chatting by the parlor fire.

PETRUCHIO.
Go, fetch them hither; if they deny to come,
Swinge me them soundly forth unto their husbands.
Away, I say, and bring them hither straight.

Go, fetch them here; if they refuse to come,
Drag them here to their husbands.
Go, I say, and bring them here straight.

[Exit KATHERINA.]

LUCENTIO.
Here is a wonder, if you talk of a wonder.

Here is a wonder, if you talk of a wonder.

HORTENSIO.
And so it is. I wonder what it bodes.

And so it is. I wonder what it means.

PETRUCHIO.
Marry, peace it bodes, and love, and quiet life,
An awful rule, and right supremacy;
And, to be short, what not that's sweet and happy.

By Mary, it means peace, and love, and quiet life,
A respected rule, and correct supremacy;
And, to be short, nothing but sweetness and
happiness.

BAPTISTA.
Now fair befall thee, good Petruchio!

Now may goodness happen to you, good
Petruchio!

The wager thou hast won; and I will add
Unto their losses twenty thousand crowns;
Another dowry to another daughter,

You have won your bet; and I will add
Onto their losses twenty thousand crowns;
Another dowry as if she were yet another
daughter,

For she is chang'd, as she had never been.

For she has been changed, as she never had been.

PETRUCHIO.
Nay, I will win my wager better yet,
And show more sign of her obedience,
Her new-built virtue and obedience.
See where she comes, and brings your froward wives
As prisoners to her womanly persuasion.

No, I will win the bet even better yet,
And show more evidence of her obedience,
Her newly built virtue and obedience.
See where she comes, and brings your rude wives
As prisoners to her womanly persuasion.

[Re-enter KATHERINA with BIANCA and WIDOW.]

Katherine, that cap of yours becomes you not:
Off with that bauble, throw it underfoot.

Katherine, that cap of yours does not flatter you:
Take off that decoration, throw it to your feet.

[KATHERINA pulls off her cap and throws it down.]

WIDOW.
Lord, let me never have a cause to sigh
Till I be brought to such a silly pass!

Lord, let me never have a reason to sigh
Until I have been brought to such a silly situation!

BIANCA.
Fie! what a foolish duty call you this?

Fie! What foolish duty do you call this?

LUCENTIO.
I would your duty were as foolish too;
The wisdom of your duty, fair Bianca,
Hath cost me a hundred crowns since supper-time!

I wish your duty was as foolish too;
The wisdom of your duty, beautiful Bianca,
Has cost me a hundred crowns since suppertime!

BIANCA.
The more fool you for laying on my duty.

The more fool you for counting on my duty.

PETRUCHIO.
Katherine, I charge thee, tell these headstrong women

Katherine, I command you, tell these headstrong
women

What duty they do owe their lords and husbands.

What duty they do owe their lords and husbands.

WIDOW.

Come, come, you're mocking; we will have no telling.

PETRUCHIO.
Come on, I say; and first begin with her.

WIDOW.
She shall not.

PETRUCHIO.
I say she shall: and first begin with her.

KATHERINA.
Fie, fie! unknit that threatening unkind brow,

And dart not scornful glances from those eyes
To wound thy lord, thy king, thy governor:
It blots thy beauty as frosts do bite the meads,

Confounds thy fame as whirlwinds shake fair buds,

And in no sense is meet or amiable.
A woman mov'd is like a fountain troubled,
Muddy, ill-seeming, thick, bereft of beauty;
And while it is so, none so dry or thirsty

Will deign to sip or touch one drop of it.

Thy husband is thy lord, thy life, thy keeper,
Thy head, thy sovereign; one that cares for thee,
And for thy maintenance commits his body
To painful labour both by sea and land,
To watch the night in storms, the day in cold,
Whilst thou liest warm at home, secure and safe;
And craves no other tribute at thy hands
But love, fair looks, and true obedience;
Too little payment for so great a debt.
Such duty as the subject owes the prince,
Even such a woman oweth to her husband;

And when she is froward, peevish, sullen, sour,
And not obedient to his honest will,
What is she but a foul contending rebel
And graceless traitor to her loving lord?--
I am asham'd that women are so simple
To offer war where they should kneel for peace,
Or seek for rule, supremacy, and sway,
When they are bound to serve, love, and obey.
Why are our bodies soft and weak and smooth,
Unapt to toll and trouble in the world,

Come, come, you're mocking; we will have no telling.

Come on, I say; and first begin with her.

She shall not.

I say she shall: and first begin with her.

Enough, enough! Smooth out that threatening unkind face,
And do not send scornful glances from those eyes
To wound your lord, your king, your ruler:
It upsets your beauty the way frosts damage the flowers,
Makes you look bad the way whirlwinds shake pretty buds,
And in no way is appropriate or pleasing.
An agitated woman is like a troubled fountain,
Muddy, ugly, thick, without beauty;
And while it is like that, no one, no matter how dry or thirsty
Will bring themselves to sip or touch one drop of it.
Your husband is your lord, your life, you keeper,
Your head, your royal; one that cares for you,
And for your sake and welfare uses his body
In painful labor in both sea and land,
To watch the night in storms, the day in cold,
While you lie warm and home, secure and safe;
And wants no other repayment from your hands
But love, sweet looks, and true obedience;
Too little payment for so great a debt.
Such duty as the subject owes the prince,
Is the same as what a omwan owes to her husband;
And when she is rude, grumpy, sullen, sour,
And not obedient to his honest will,
What is she but a disgusting, fighting rebel
And graceless traitor to her loving lord?--
I am ashamed that women are so foolish
To offer war where they should kneel for peace,
Or try for rule, dominance, and influence,
When they are supposed to serve, love, and obey.
Why are our bodies soft and weak and smooth,
Not suitable for hard work and trouble in the world,

But that our soft conditions and our hearts
Should well agree with our external parts?
Come, come, you froward and unable worms!
My mind hath been as big as one of yours,
My heart as great, my reason haply more,
To bandy word for word and frown for frown;
But now I see our lances are but straws,
Our strength as weak, our weakness past compare,
That seeming to be most which we indeed least are.
Then vail your stomachs, for it is no boot,
And place your hands below your husband's foot:
In token of which duty, if he please,
My hand is ready; may it do him ease.

But except our soft conditions and our hearts
Should agree with our outside parts?
Come, come, you rude and incapable worms!
My mind has been as big as one of yours,
My heart as big, my reason perhaps more,
To fight with word for word and frown for frown;
But now I see our lances are only straws,
Our strength as weak, our weakness past compare,
That seems to be most what we indeed are least.
Then cover your stomachs, for it is no boot,
And place your hands below your husband's foot:
In token of which duty, if he please,
My hand is ready; may it do him ease.

PETRUCHIO.
Why, there's a wench! Come on, and kiss me, Kate.

Why, there's a girl! Come on, and kiss me, Kate.

LUCENTIO.
Well, go thy ways, old lad, for thou shalt ha't.

Well, go your way, old lad, for you shall have it.

VINCENTIO.
'Tis a good hearing when children are toward.

It is good when children are coming.

LUCENTIO.
But a harsh hearing when women are froward.

But bad when women are rude.

PETRUCHIO.
Come, Kate, we'll to bed.
We three are married, but you two are sped.
'Twas I won the wager,

Come, Kate, we will go to bed.
We three are married, but you two need to go.
It was I who won the wager,

[To LUCENTIO.]

though you hit the white;
And being a winner, God give you good night!

though you came close;
And being a winner, God give you good night!

[Exeunt PETRUCHIO and KATHERINA.]

HORTENSIO.
Now go thy ways; thou hast tam'd a curst shrew.

Now go on your way; you have tamed a cursed
shrew.

LUCENTIO.
'Tis a wonder, by your leave, she will be tam'd so.

It's amazing, if you will, that she was tamed like
that.

[Exeunt.]

Printed in Great Britain
by Amazon